Incidental Music

NOVELS BY FRANÇOISE SAGAN:

Bonjour Tristesse
A Certain Smile
Those Without Shadows
Aimez-vous Brahms?
The Wonderful Clouds
La Chamade
The Heartkeeper
A Few Hours of Sunlight
Scars on the Soul
Lost Profile
The Unmade Bed
The Painted Lady

Françoise Sagan

Incidental Music

Translated by
C.J. Richards

E. P. DUTTON, INC.   NEW YORK

*Published in the United States by
E. P. Dutton, Inc., 2 Park Avenue, New York, N.Y. 10016*

*Library of Congress Cataloging in Publication Data
Sagan, Françoise,
Incidental music.
Translation of: Musiques de scènes.
Contents: The cat and the casino—Aftermath of a duel—
La Futura—[etc.]
1. Sagan, Françoise—Translations, English. I. Title.
PQ2633.U74M87 1983   843'.914   83-20590*

ISBN: 0-525-24213-9

*Published simultaneously in Canada by
Fitzhenry & Whiteside Limited, Toronto.*

Designed by Nancy Etheredge

10 9 8 7 6 5 4 3 2 1
First Edition

To my friend Jean-Jaques Pauvert

Contents

Incidental Music

The Cat
and the Casino

Angela di Stefano, who had spent the morning shouting in vain for her cat, Rascal, vanished in the narrow streets of the old quarter of Nice. It was now three o'clock in the afternoon and, for September, hideously hot. Whatever the charms of neighborhood females, Rascal did not usually forget his siesta or his food. Angela, who doted on him, had become increasingly worried. Her husband, Giuseppe, had gone bowling as he did every Saturday afternoon. Her neighbors were taking their siestas on brass beds behind the customary array of gaily

I

colored wash that hung from their windows. Angela, a shawl on her head to shield her from the burning sun, walked softly so as not to disturb them, whispering hoarsely: "Rascal! Rascal!" as she went from doorway to doorway.

Angela di Stefano, at thirty-two, was a beautiful woman, her soft appealing body in marked contrast to the firm line of her jaw. The austerity of her features, product of her Corsican origins, had discouraged would-be suitors, a subject of occasional and unwelcome teasing by Giuseppe.

Still no sign of Rascal and she had to get to the bank before four in order to make the monthly five-hundred-franc mortgage payment on their house. Like a good husband, Giuseppe had given her his paycheck the night before, and she wanted to put this hard-earned money into safekeeping as quickly as possible.

Suddenly there was a streak of gray behind a wall. "Rascal!" she cried, then opened the gate of a small garden—that of the fair Elena. Elena had been their neighbor for ten years and, since her widowhood, the object, without proof, of much gossip. Still walking quietly, Angela took a couple of steps forward and caught a glimpse of Rascal poised tauntingly on the windowsill. She called him once more before making a move to catch him. He darted her an infuriating come-hither look and jumped into the house. Angela, leaning on the shutter to steady herself as she reached inside to grab him, saw her handsome Giuseppe asleep in Elena's arms. She backed away, her heart pounding, terrified he might have seen her.

It was only when she was in the street again, walking fast, that her shock turned to anger. She ought to have known, the whole neighborhood must know, even Rascal knew. . . . So that was where Giuseppe went bowling on certain Saturdays! How long had this been going on?

She would go back to her mother, to her island where decent people lived. Infidelity was not for women like her. For ten years she had looked after Giuseppe di Stefano, his house, his business, his meals, his bed. For ten years she had done his bidding, tried to please him; and for what? So that he could lie to her night and day, all the while thinking of someone else!

She found herself on the Promenade des Anglais, where she normally never went. Nonetheless she moved forward unhesitatingly toward the water's edge, as though she had only to continue walking to reach her parents' house without so much as getting her feet wet.

A shrill whistle saved her from being run over. She turned abruptly and saw she was in front of a large white building, the casino. Here, it was rumored, foreigners came to lose their fortunes; even the men from her neighborhood ventured in only timidly. She saw a blonde woman, plainly much older than she, in linen slacks, heard her laugh with the doorman before vanishing into the dark interior. Something about this darkness drew Angela; it was cool and dim, in sharp contrast to the dazzling sunshine beating down on the sidewalk. Without thinking, she followed the woman up the steps.

Angela was simply dressed but she had style and the doorman did not hesitate to escort her to the gaming room. Here a man dressed in black, after asking for identification, inquired how many chips she wanted. Angela moved as in a dream; the only clues she had as to what to do next were scenes she remembered from television. She had never in her entire life gambled for even one franc nor played any game more complicated than Russian Bank. In a perfectly steady voice she asked for five hundred francs' worth of chips, handed over Giuseppe's beautiful clean bill, and received in exchange five small round objects, which she was apparently expected to place on the green table a little farther down. A few preoccupied players, wilting from the heat, had already crowded around it, and she was thus afforded the opportunity to watch and learn from them for at least a few minutes without attracting attention.

She clutched her chips so tightly she could feel the sweat collecting on the palm of her hand. Nervously she shifted them to her other hand and furtively wiped off the dampness. In the hush that

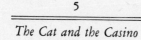
greeted the stopping of the little bouncing ball she took one of the shiny objects and placed it firmly on number eight. She had been married on August the eighth, in Nice, and she lived at No. 8, rue des Petites Ecuries.

"Rien ne va plus," said a languid man in evening clothes. He tossed back the little ball, which began to spin frantically before falling gracefully into a small black compartment too far from Angela for her to make out the number.

"Le numéro huit," said the man in a tired voice. *"Huit en plein,"* he added after surveying the table. He lined up another ten or twelve chips and, after looking around the table once more, placed them in front of Angela. He then mentioned another sum (which seemed astronomical to her) and looked at her questioningly.

"Number eight," Angela said again in a steady voice. She felt at ease, as though guided by an unknown spirit, and wondered fleetingly at the speed with which the picture of Giuseppe and Elena had faded. All she could see now was the little ball.

Surprised, the croupier said: "The maximum is two thousand on a single number."

She nodded wordlessly, without understanding, so the croupier placed a pile of her chips on number eight and handed her the others, which she stacked up automatically.

People had gathered and were examining her with some curiosity. Neither the expression on her face nor her attitude gave any hint of the enormity of her folly. Here she was in September, in Nice's summer casino, gambling away two thousand francs on a single number.

After a second's hesitation, the croupier said: *"Faites vos jeux!"* The lady in slacks put ten francs next to Angela's shining stack and the ball went round again. After some bouncing and pinging it stopped. Silence, then an apparently shocked murmuring that revived Angela, who had closed her eyes—from fatigue rather than surprise, or so her heavy eyelids implied.

"Le huit," said the croupier in a voice she thought less cheerful than before. Turning toward Angela, who had remained cool, impassive, he bowed and said: "My compliments, Madame. We owe you sixty-six thousand francs. Please follow me."

She was surrounded by men who were partly disgruntled, partly obsequious. They led her to a counter where another man, with pale eyes, counted out some chips that were much larger and squarer than the first batch. Angela said nothing. There was a buzzing in her ears and she felt dizzy.

"How much does all this come to?" she asked, pointing to the pile.

When the man replied, "Sixty-six thousand francs, Madame, that is six million six hundred thousand old francs," she put out her hand for support. He seated her very courteously, ordered her

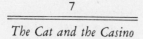

a brandy, and handed it to her with the same icy courtesy.

"Could I have it in cash?" Angela asked after the warmth of the brandy had penetrated.

"Of course." He plunged his hands back into the drawer and took out a mountain of bills: yellow ones, like the one Giuseppe had entrusted to her care that very morning. He even helped her stuff them into her bag.

"You don't care to gamble again, Madame?" It was not even a question, for it was quite plain to him that this was the first and last time Angela di Stefano would ever set foot in a casino. She shook her head, said, "Thank you very much," and walked out with the same firm step she had used when walking in.

The sun revived her. Her eyes took in the sea, the Promenade des Anglais, the cars, the ancient palm trees. Then she remembered that she was a woman betrayed. She sat down at the first cafe she came to—the first time Angela di Stefano had ever gone alone to a cafe—placed her bag securely between her ankles, and in a faint voice asked the waiter for a raspberry ice. Then she began to think.

A short young man dressed in beige, who had followed her from the casino, tried to strike up a conversation by offering her a cigarette. She brushed him aside wordlessly but with so eloquent a gesture that perhaps for the first time in his life the young parasite, accustomed to hanging out around women and casinos, gave up on the first try; he knew a stone wall when he ran into it.

After he had gone she was at last left to her own thoughts. She examined one by one three or four schemes that had sprung into her mind.

The first was to deposit the wad of yellow-backs in the bank as soon as possible—but that would have been into Giuseppe's account, and because Giuseppe had betrayed her she had to leave him.

The second was to hire a boat and go straight back to her parents.

The third was (just like in a novel) to take a taxi, drive to the house, pick up Rascal and her belongings, and leave five hundred francs along with a heartbreaking note to Giuseppe, then drive to the port, etc.

The fourth was more elaborate: to go to one of the big department stores, drape herself in filmy red silk, cover herself with jewelry, rent a horse-and-carriage, and arrive home at full gallop, dazzling her neighbors and tossing candy to children along the way. Or she could hire a couple of thugs (there must be some around) to beat up Elena. Or she could hire a car with a tall chauffeur in a gray uniform, who would deliver a note to a neighbor asking her to give him Rascal and pack a suitcase with Angela's belongings.

All these dizzying possibilities, combined with

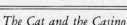

the injudicious mixture of cognac and raspberry ice, sent waves of nausea over her. For such a long time now her life had been free of uncertainties; she had known exactly what would take place every moment of the day, week, even year. No choices had been required of her in such a long time that suddenly the picture of Giuseppe in Elena's arms became almost a steadying thought. This was real, it had taken place, she could do nothing about it now; it was beyond recall. Uncertainty and panic lay in ambush in the bag at her feet.

Without that money she would have gone home, hurled insults at Giuseppe, threatened to leave him. She might even have left him for a while until he came, full of remorse, to find her on her island. Without that bag of money life would have remained simple, unruffled, and in the long run sweet: she loved Giuseppe and, although she was aware that he had a roving eye, she also knew that he loved her. Whenever he happened to have a few extra francs, he always gave them to her. She was the one who had insisted on buying the old house on the rue des Petites Ecuries. It was he who kept promising her the red silk dress; she had never really wanted it. And the Saturday before it had been her neighbor's son, not Giuseppe, who had spent the afternoon with Elena.

The trouble was that now there was a whole bagful of alternatives at her feet. She need not be merely a wife betrayed, obliged to come face to face with a penitent husband; she could be a wealthy woman leaving behind her a heartbroken man. Giuseppe was a mason, a handsome man, true, but no longer in his prime, and he did not earn very much. If she left he might not find another.

Dusk was gathering slowly on the gray and blonde sea that had become satiny smooth. Angela was afraid that Giuseppe might start to worry. Perhaps he would think that she had been robbed on her way to the bank. He would certainly never dream that she was here in this cafe on this bright avenue with thousands of francs at her feet, or that she might walk away and never see him again. What would he and Rascal do when eight o'clock came around? They would be waiting for her at the door, like the good-for-nothings they were, unable even to find the makings for supper: oil, flour, sausage, wine. No. This could never be. Even if she did decide to leave, she could not see herself in a sumptuous hotel consuming lobster and champagne, picking out pastries brought her by the headwaiter. She really hadn't much use for the money; anything it bought would leave a bitter taste. She simply was not up to making choices. She had neither seen enough television shows nor read enough books to guide her along these unknown paths. Nor ever dreamed about anyone except Giuseppe.

She got to her feet, went back into the casino, and was lucky enough to run into the man with pale eyes, the one who had given her the brandy. He recognized her right away. She drew him into a dark corner and whispered her request.

"What did you say?" he asked. He had spoken loudly, his face reddening as people turned round to look at them. She drew him closer, began to whisper again, and all at once he seemed to understand.

"You want me to take it back? But I'm not allowed to, Madame."

He summoned another man, also in evening clothes, and the three of them whispered. The two men had a strange look on their faces; they suddenly looked younger, almost childlike. Anyone overhearing them would have been surprised to learn that the two croupiers and the handsome woman were talking about the relative merits of two charities: the Merchantmen's Aid Society and the Brothers of the Poor. They ended up going into the office. Angela took out her money and was given a check, which she endorsed to the Society of Saint Vincent. She signed "Angela di Stefano." It was plain this was the first and probably last time she would ever sign a check. She left then, her head held high as she passed nervous men and women in evening dress entering the casino, for this was the hour when the serious gaming began. The two croupiers escorted her with such marked courtesy and deference that the elegant ladies turned to look at her, a puzzled expression on their faces.

FRANÇOISE SAGAN

She went home; there she found Rascal and Giuseppe both seated, one in the other's lap, in front of the television.

"You're awfully late," grumbled Giuseppe.

She mumbled as she began rattling her pots and pans: "Yes, the bank took a long time, and I met a cousin from Bastia."

Giuseppe, who was feeling a bit guilty and who had had a most trying time getting rid of the horrible scent of cologne in which Elena dowsed herself, gently patted her as she went by. He was sleepy. A neighbor outside was singing off-key and the cat was already purring at the aroma issuing from the frying pan.

A very pleasant Saturday, thought Giuseppe. A man has a right to a little fling every so often. Women don't understand.

Aftermath of a Duel

The winter of 1883 in Austria came early. The cold weather started in September, driving game back to their dens earlier than usual. This cut short Baron von Tenck's hunting. He returned to Vienna ten days before he was expected. There he found in his wife's bed Lieutenant Serge Olevitch of the First Guard. Baron von Tenck made this painful discovery at eight o'clock in the morning on a Tuesday. That very afternoon the duel was fixed by his seconds and those of the young man for the following Wednesday morning. Baroness Ilse von Tenck spent the evening alternately weeping and bathing her eyes with camomile. Baron von Tenck oiled his pistols once more and added a few codicils to his will. Wisely, the four seconds went to bed early. Only the young officer, Serge Olevitch, behaved in a less conventional manner; he was scared out of his wits.

Serge Olevitch was the scion of an old Austro-Hungarian family. He had been brought up piously and strictly. He was moderately good-looking and almost intelligent. He enjoyed life but did not indulge in excesses; he was good-natured and cheerful; in short, he had everything to make him happy. Even his cowardice had cast only a slight shadow on his childhood, for a private tutor had preserved him from the gibes and beatings that were normally the lot of Austrian schoolboys and, having sisters only, he had not had to put up with the tyranny of an older brother. His innate good nature had made it easy for him, later, to establish pleasant relations with even the most brutish members of his regiment. There was nothing about him to arouse envy or hatred, for he was a good fellow. It was the purest chance that brought him to Baroness von Tenck's bed after a ball at which he had drunk too much.

The forty-year-old Ilse von Tenck was notorious throughout Viennese society for her appetites; even her husband was aware of them. Had the baron not returned to town earlier than usual, Serge

Aftermath of a Duel

Olevitch could easily have become, indeed re-mained, the discreet lover of the handsome Aus-trian lady—without arousing criticism. But even the most accommodating husband cannot evade a duty imposed by irrefutable evidence: a naked wife in the arms of a naked young man in the conjugal bed, and witnessed by a footman. A trip to the field of honor was the unavoidable consequence. Baron von Tenck, who was not the least bloodthirsty, was desolated by the course of action forced upon him, for he was both the best shot in the Austrian Empire and the least attentive of husbands.

Serge Olevitch paced up and down in his room, his shirt open despite the cold, occasionally glancing, stricken and shamefaced, at his mirror. He enjoyed looking at the reflection of a healthy, vigorous young man, but he was ashamed of the expression of terror that almost disfigured him. Von Tenck was going to kill him. Since the baron was the offended party, he would be the first to shoot, and he would not miss. Serge Olevitch was going to his death because of unseasonably early clouds in an autumn sky; he was going to die for the sake of a woman whom neither her husband nor he particu-larly desired. His death would be pointless. That straight nose, luxuriant head of hair, tanned skin, and strongly beating heart would soon (almost im-mediately) be nothing but a limp heap to be hur-riedly buried. The young man in the mirror wore an expression of such horror that he groaned out loud. The sound startled him; it was like that of an animal at bay.

He simply had to find a way out. Running away would be tantamount to suicide; he would be dishonored, forsaken by family and friends, disinherited. There would be nothing left of a once happy life. Since flight was out of the question, he had to find some other way out of fighting this duel. For a fleeting moment he toyed with the absurd plan of stealing up to the Von Tenck residence and, under cover of darkness, silently creeping into the baron's bedroom to murder him. But the murderer would soon be found out and the dishonor would be just as great as if he had fled. Better to be shot than executed. There seemed to be nothing to keep Baron von Tenck from going, at dawn, to the banks of the Danube, nothing to prevent his killing Serge. Unless. . . .

The sweat, which had been pouring down the young man's body, suddenly dried up. Serge Olevitch turned from the mirror and sat on the bed. *Unless* he himself was unable to be present at the encounter. After all, he could be assassinated by a third party; assassinated . . . or almost assassinated. All of Serge's future was contained in that absurd, casual little word "almost." The clock struck two; there was not a second to be lost. He knew that the "almost" would only postpone the duel; that any sort of accident would grant him only a month or so of grace, but during that precious time he knew he would hit upon a solution. Time, he needed time. Above all the clock must stop chiming away the hours leading him to the grave. This dawn simply could not be his last one. The sun must shine on him as well the day after. Serge Olevitch flung open his window and jumped feetfirst from the third floor.

The waters of the small town of Thuringe were not specifically recommended for bone problems. Four sulphur sources, an alley bordered by two rows of royal elms, and three elegant old hotels were its sole attraction. Therefore the arrival of young Serge Olevitch at the Hunter Gasthaus surprised both those taking the cure and the local inhabitants, among the latter a most respected lady, Hannette von Tenck, owner of ten thousand acres east of Thuringe and of the most beautiful mansion in the town, but most importantly the only sister of the wronged baron.

At fifty, Hannette von Tenck was a confirmed spinster. A number of suitors, attracted more perhaps by her fortune than by her charms, had been unable to lead her to the altar. Tall and dessicated, with vividly red hair and a haughty expression, the initial sentiment she inspired was respect, even awe, not love. To Serge Olevitch, however, she represented the only means by which the baron might, indeed must, be prevented from fighting his duel. And on this beautiful winter morning, as she came to the doors of the Church of San Joachim, which were blocked by the young lieutenant in his wheelchair, he thought her the very incarnation of beauty, even more than beauty, of life itself. Her red hair conjured up the warmth of fire, her erect figure was like a bulwark, her age promised security. It was not precisely the thought of sharing the baroness's bed that excited the young man's ardor, but it was a prospect that repelled him far less than that of a certain dawn on the outskirts of Vienna, a black pistol aimed at him. No promiscuity could be worse than lying in a cemetery, no physical contact more repellent than no contact at all.

If feelings are to be judged by their intensity as well as by their nature, Serge Olevitch became the most ardent lover in the whole of the Germanic empire. The chaste Hannette, who until his arrival had been unaccustomed to such gallantries, was showered with letters, flowers, attentions. In the few moments she could spare from deer hunting (Hannette was an accomplished horsewoman who spent most of her waking hours in the saddle), she became concerned about the handsome young man's assiduity. She made inquiries and learned with pleasure and surprise that he was wealthy, and with no surprise and no pleasure that he had been the lover of her sister-in-law. It never occurred to Hannette that the repeated attentions her family was receiving were anything but an unfortunate co-incidence—indeed she was beginning to find it a

most unfortunate coincidence for the lieutenant.
Both she and her brother had been trained by the
same master-at-arms, so she was well aware that the
baron was a crack shot. Stricken at the thought of
seeing Serge dead, she spoke to him about the duel
and realized that he shared her forebodings. She
believed at once that the young man was guileless
—on the principle that people who are about to die
don't lie. His seeming moral grace appealed to her,
as did his conversational charms. Not for an instant
did she suspect the real reason for his apparent infatuation. In the von Tenck family the word "fear"
had no meaning; it was nothing but a combination
of letters. Yet it was fear, not adoration, that caused
Serge Olevitch to speak haltingly; it was panic that
made his eyes dim with tears.

Until now, Hannette von Tenck had had only
the most ceremonial ideas about marriage. Her own
needs were more than satisfied every day by eight
hours in the saddle. In the past, whenever her hand
had been solicited in marriage, she had seen herself
in a bridal dress on the arm of her suitor in the
Church of San Joachim, and every time the vision
had struck her as absurd. Now, perhaps because of
her admirer's doomed future, she felt less like
laughing. She viewed his hasty wooing and dread of
a refusal first with curiosity, then with tolerance,
and finally with compassion.

One winter evening after having spent the afternoon on horseback and noticing with approval

how well the convalescent rode, she spoke to him frankly. "The only obstacle to our marriage," she said, "would be my brother. And I daresay he won't want to kill his brother-in-law." Then, neighing affectionately, she added, "And I should never forgive him. On the other hand, leaving a duel unfinished is dishonorable."

"I should gladly sacrifice even my honor for our love," Serge Olevitch stated firmly. The proud damsel was touched by this outburst of feeling; only later did it occur to her that it was, after all, her brother's honor that had been at stake.

"Oh well," she said, shrugging her powerful shoulders and flicking off the leaves of a green birch branch with her riding crop, "my brother has killed enough men. He doesn't really like blood. And even if he wanted to he couldn't possibly dispose of all the young studs who have mounted my sister-in-law. Don't argue," she continued in response to the weak and gallant protestations of the young man.

And so she exchanged her riding crop for a goose quill and, after allowing Serge Olevitch to kiss her hand for the first time, she put it to work writing the news of her forthcoming marriage to her brother.

In Vienna the baron, who had half-forgotten his duel (remembering the date only as one remembers the date of Palm Sunday or Easter), was quite delighted by this somewhat late betrothal. He normally viewed with some misgivings his sister's return to Vienna: unable to expend her energies riding, she used to insist on spending interminably dull evenings with him. And he was surprised to learn that her fiancé was wealthy.

What a dull-witted young man, he thought, and made no attempt to find an explanation for this inexplicable marriage. When Baroness von Tenck heard the news, she shed a few tears, dampened a few handkerchiefs, and emptied a few flasks. But her native optimism surfaced and she talked herself into believing that this was a daring ruse on the part of her lover; in a complete turmoil and carried away at the idea of incest, she gave herself to an embassy attaché.

A short time later, a hunt put the finishing touches to our hero's reputation. While the whips were rounding up the deer, the engaged couple, who had imprudently dismounted, took a few steps along a narrow path. Whether it was Hannette's penetrating laugh or the distant sound of the horn that aroused him, a large boar charged the couple. Hannette was already running back to her horse to fetch her hunting knife when Serge Olevitch, who had been walking in front of her, stopped, frozen with terror. This is all so silly, he thought fuzzily as he stood transfixed, a barrier between his nimble-footed fiancée and the raging beast. He then toppled over in a dead faint. The boar was already upon him and Olevitch would doubtless have been horribly mangled had not something, probably Hannette's fiery red hair, suddenly made the animal change course. In any event, a few moments later Hannette, on her knees, tears in her eyes, beheld the man who had made a rampart of his body, who on foot had braved for her the charge of a two-hundred-pound boar. The blood of the von Tencks would have been in good company, she thought, and for the first and only time regretted fleetingly that there would be no little von Tenck-Olevitches.

Hannette was not a romantic. There was no nonsense about her, as the inhabitants of Thuringe were well aware, so that when she had given a brief but precise account of her fiancé's exploit, the whole town was struck with as much admiration as surprise. To risk death for the sake of a helpless woman was understandable, but for Hannette von Tenck—well, she did not qualify! Consequently Serge Olevitch was accorded the respect owed a brave man as well as the somewhat more nebulous deference engendered by foolhardy behavior. In any event he enjoyed the dimly fearful and quite unexpected admiration bestowed upon him.

Although the boar had scarcely touched him and he had fallen no farther than the length of his own height, the shock had had a profound effect upon him. He was still a coward, but he felt less ashamed of it now. He kept repeating to himself that this was all so silly, really silly, wryly aware that this thought could so easily have been his last one. A feeling of detachment characteristic of the English but totally alien to his native Westphalia, indeed to all of Prussia, filled his soul, as he gradually adjusted to his new reputation.

Three months later, steeped in this feeling of beatific detachment, he married Hannette, her cheeks red from sunburn rather than maidenly modesty, and he embraced with genuine warmth and not a shadow of rancor the man who could so easily have become his murderer.

Life in Thuringe was uneventful and, having given up the army in order to devote himself to his wife's and to his own property, Serge Olevitch, who loved the country and was not averse to an occasional bit of philandering, might well have spent endlessly happy days there had not an unexpected twist of fate wiped out that possibility.

Hannette von Tenck had been a fanatic horsewoman. After a wedding night during which Serge Olevitch had acquitted himself with honor if not with éclat, Hannette von Tenck had become insatiably aroused. Her amorous desires became as unbridled as her equestrian passion. The bed became her saddle; the forests around Thuringe no longer echoed with her tallyhos, but far more piercing cries rent the air of the large mansion. The fears of her brother had not been unfounded. The impetuous von Tenck blood, aroused so late, forced the unfortunate Serge Olevitch into dizzying excesses to which his somewhat placid temperament was unequal. Love, which had been the means of his escape from death, was now leading him straight back into its jaws. Pale, liverish, subsisting on red meat and the treacherous muscat wine of the Westphalian vineyards, Lieutenant Serge Olevitch could see his existence gradually slipping away behind a veil of red disheveled hair that showed no signs of turning gray. Six months after his marriage, he took to his bed with a cough. The doctors summoned from Vienna diagnosed consumption. Hannette's grief was painful to behold. She tried at first, upon the advice of her brother and her friends and while her husband was resting, to recapture her past pleasure in riding. Unfortunately, the galloping reminded her of a kind she had enjoyed more, and exertions in the saddle were never equal to her energy.

One spring afternoon, while she was riding heavyhearted through the countryside, accompanied by her faithful whip, she committed the imprudence of complaining to that rustic. He misunderstood her, or possibly understood her too well. Thus was the handsome twenty-five-year-old lieutenant of the First Regiment of the Guards cuckolded by a wife of fifty and a country bumpkin.

Unaware of all this, Olevitch had, by the autumn, regained a little color and, although thin, was seen the first Sunday in October leaving high Mass at the Church of San Joachim on the arm of his bride.

Aftermath of a Duel

And indeed, after two months of rest, the white meat of chicken, and port wine, Serge Olevitch thought he was cured. Hannette would sleep beside him peacefully, her powerful breathing occasionally shaking the bed's canopy but without her ever attempting any of her earlier furious attacks, the remembrance of which still made his blood run cold. There were moments when he wondered if those ghastly nights, those terrifying face-to-face combats that had so often sent him flying from the bed, had not been figments of his imagination. As he thought back on such scenes, the young man silently crossed himself in the dark, for there had been moments during that near-fatal spring when he would have preferred the sight of that charging boar to the approach of Hannette in her nightclothes, ogling him appraisingly as soon as they were in bed.

The couple was due to return to Vienna and, having recovered his health, the young man could even envisage without revulsion some commonplace affair with an Opera ballerina. He said to himself he would choose someone light, airy, diaphanous, transparent. These adjectives effortlessly followed one another, stopping only when a sudden groan from the bed indicated that Hannette was turning over in her sleep. The dear woman. . . . Now that her initial frenzy had passed, she continued to show him affection and did not even insist that he accompany her during those exhausting rides!

It was with some difficulty that he persuaded

her it was time to return to the capital. He assured her there were lovely bridle paths in the woods of Sprau, that they would certainly find some nobleman as enthusiastic as she about that noble sport who would gladly escort her during her outings on horseback. Serge Olevitch's words were well-intentioned, but fell wide of the mark. He did not realize that the delicate and blasé Viennese possessed neither the cool nor the warmth of the Thuringe peasantry, and that he was beckoning his bride to famine.

The first ball given by the newlyweds attracted all that was aristocratic and brilliant in Viennese society. The wealth of the bride and the certainty that she would provide good music and good food were, however, less of an attraction than the desire to inspect the odd couple. It was a good party. The guests noted with some amusement that throughout the evening the dashing Serge Olevitch, resplendent in his black evening clothes, was the quarry of his sister-in-law, Baroness von Tenck. In the meantime Hannette, her leathery face pink and wreathed in smiles, was waltzing energetically. To the amusement of some of the guests, the elderly, fragile Baron Turnhauh, who had incautiously asked her for a dance, suddenly lost his balance, his monocle in full flight as she thrust herself vigorously against him. With great care she shepherded him to an armchair.

Truth to tell, Hannette's gaiety was heart-warming to see. With her ruddy complexion, muscular neck, and robust laughter more usually found on the hunting field than in a ballroom, she offered a welcome contrast to the frail and willowy Viennese noblewomen, pasty-faced from a summer spent in the shade. From time to time she and her handsome bridegroom would exchange loverlike looks that, over all, made a good impression. A few dowagers and some mean-spirited young women made nasty remarks, but on the whole the first ball given by the Olevitches was a success.

It was noticed, however, that a number of guests, after waltzing with the mistress of the house, wore a somewhat startled look; they would pause with knitted brow, then look around uncertainly before sallying bravely forth again onto the dance floor, shrugging their shoulders. Baron Cornelius von Strass, for one, said to himself that he must have been dreaming. Surely poor Hannette, so virtuous, could not possibly have asked him, coolly, between two polkas to . . . "take a tumble" with her? And she had phrased it somewhat more crudely!

Meanwhile Dr. Zimenatt, the eminent physician, was telling himself he must be mad to think he had felt Hannette's hand on his . . . !?

Still in doubt, the gentlemen did not dare exchange notes with each other and discuss their impressions, especially since their wives were already gaping and gossiping. "How appalling," they sighed, "that Hannette, once so virtuous, only just married, should already be unfaithful to her handsome husband." There was general distress that so dashing a man should be tied to such a strange creature.

And indeed, Serge Olevitch would have had no trouble in choosing a mistress from among the most beautiful and desirable women in Vienna. But, contrary to all expectations, he showed no inclination to do so. He had eyes only for Hannette and presented a wooden countenance to all coquettish looks.

His bride, on the other hand, so openly solicited the men she encountered that she was thought to have completely forgotten how to behave in polite society—possibly a result of her lengthy sojourn in the country. Her overtures could not have been more blatant had she wanted to jump into bed with the first available male. People thought her attitude must be misleading, but the young Aloysus von Schimmel deemed otherwise one fine evening in December.

Aloysus von Schimmel was a somewhat degenerate young man born into an old, old family. Perhaps this accounted for his consumptiveness, near-sightedness, and inability to concentrate. At twenty-seven he looked no older than fifteen. To give him a touch of sophistication, his family had had him settled in Vienna some ten years earlier. He was seldom seen anywhere except at his piano.

He was of a gloomy disposition, touchy and child-ish. His small, thin body was topped by a head of thick, curly hair of the same vivid color as Han-nette's. Having up to then spurned the advances of a number of Viennese ladies attracted by his for-tune, he suddenly came to life when he saw, re-flected in the dark wood of his piano, Hannette's fiery hair. He got up from his stool and suddenly wanted to dance, something he had done only about half a dozen times in ten years. Hannette grabbed the young sprig by the waist and they galloped off at a pace suggestive of a hunt. That evening they became known as "the carrot tops."

The contrast between the healthy, ruddy-com-plexioned von Tenck heiress and the pale, puny von Schimmel heir was striking. The only bond between them appeared to be that vividly colored hair, but they speedily forged another one. Hannette had the fun of showing him, only very shortly after she herself had discovered them, the delights of love. Aloysus, tamed, shaken up, petted, trounced, fed, indeed force-fed, began, unlike Serge, to gain in strength. In the morning the proud Hannette could be seen galloping along the bridle paths in the woods, followed by her pianist. In the evening they met over a piano score or beside a fireplace. As for afternoons, it soon became plain how they spent them. Passion raged between the two flaming heads. And still Serge Olevitch made no move.

Viennese society began to consider the situation more and more bizarre. That a handsome, wealthy young man should take it into his head to marry the ungrateful Hannette was surprising; that she should have consented to the match after twenty years of chastity and deer hunting was astonishing; but that upon their return to Vienna it was she who was unfaithful was positively scandalous. People began to gossip. Doubts were raised about the bridegroom's virility. Serge Olevitch, who was aware of this, felt compelled to prove himself. He went to the Opera in search of a dancer. Unfortunately, since Viennese men were as concerned about the constancy of their mistresses as they were unconcerned about the fidelity of their wives, Serge Olevitch had to handle the affair with kid gloves in order to avoid a duel, which would have set him back years. Thus, he was constrained to choose from among those beauties one who was not otherwise taken up—that is to say, a very plain one.

Delighted by her sudden success, the young woman could not help but boast about Serge, and soon it became impossible to ascribe the odd marital situation of the Olevitches to a pathological weakness on the part of the bridegroom.

It must also be added that Hannette, although apparently very much in love, did not indulge in the mincing ways and simperings that are bound to force an ordinary man to act like a jealous husband. She would thump her lover vigorously on the back, hail him loudly in terms that left no doubt as to the nature of their relationship. The mating habits of the two carrot tops might well have been coarsely likened to that of rabbits, but it was hard to take offense at them for it. And Olevitch took great care not to. Although he found young Aloysus's cries of pleasure tiresome, he thought himself lucky that Hannette's fancy had not lit upon a garrulous butler or an unmannerly footman. He even felt a twinge of admiration for the nervous energy that seemed to animate the young pianist. He felt sorry about the dark circles under his eyes, and made allowances for the occasional sour notes Von Schimmel struck on the keyboard. His role was simple: to see nothing.

To keep up his part in the comedy, Serge Olevitch spent the winter coughing, bumping into furniture, talking to himself out loud, ringing the doorbell instead of using his latchkey, and taking endless other precautions. The lovers would be caught together only if they wanted to be. Aloysus von Schimmel was no more anxious to have this occur than Serge was. The mere thought that he, Serge, might see them in each other's arms, that they might see him seeing them, froze his blood. If this were to happen, Serge would have to act, in other words, call the young man out, at dawn, with pistols. . . . This was Serge Olevitch's recurring nightmare.

Alas! The unavoidable can be avoided just so long. One day as he was entering his hothouse, where he had recently taken to growing orchids (Serge Olevitch had developed a passion for horticulture), he had the ill-fated idea of placing some more straw around a new shoot that was especially sensitive to the cold. There, in the gardener's domain, amid the bales of straw, he discovered Hannette and Aloysus in a close embrace, and although not entirely naked, at least partly so. "Hannette!" he groaned. Her response, more energetic but equally startled, was to let forth a pagan oath. As for the young man, he was already straightening his collar and bowing low with a courtly air that only put the finishing touches to Serge Olevitch's exasperation. He wanted to slap him in earnest, not for his misdeed, but for his clumsiness.

"Don't hit him!" cried our heroine, remembering the boar. This brought Serge Olevitch up short. He managed to look both stern and calm. He, too, bowed deeply before the somewhat unnerved couple, then stated firmly "I saw nothing" before closing the door. His heart racing but his features unruffled, he strode into his room. Here he locked himself in with strict orders not to be disturbed. This way, that presumptuous young puppy will have time to calm down, he thought to himself. Hannette would be the only one he need persuade of the wisdom of his decision.

She was annoyed at the turn of events, and this sobered her up, for she had been wholly intoxicated by the irrepressible ardor of young Aloysus. But by now the novelty of stolen embraces in out-of-the-way corners had worn off, and she was beginning to long for the simple vigor of the forester. Also, pastoral peace and the benevolent silence of nature were more appealing to her than the noises of the city.

Nonetheless, this adventure had provided her with a measure of satisfaction; a fillip had been added to daily living. It was almost like a French novel: she was looking forward to acting out a scene of repentance at the feet of her darling Serge Olevitch. As a sign of affliction, she let her hair down. Thrusting aside the valet and treading firmly forward—for even when she wore bedroom slippers her footsteps resounded as if she wore boots—she burst in on her husband.

Serge Olevitch was in his dressing gown smoking a fine cigar. After a momentary hesitation, she decided it would be more fitting to sit opposite him than to be at his feet.

"A most regrettable incident," she began in her beautiful deep voice. "I am truly sorry. The hothouse idea was not mine."

Serge Olevitch said nothing. Hannette surmised that pride, rather than grief, was the reason for his silence. She had heard about the homely Opera dancer.

"Oh, come on," she said, "it was nothing. We could have a smallish sort of duel—surely you wouldn't be mean enough to cripple a mere boy—then we could return to Thuringe for a few months to get away from the gossip."

"It's out of the question," Serge Olevitch answered. "A duel is out of the question."

A rush of blood empurpled his companion's already florid complexion, but Serge Olevitch swept away the ignominious thought entering his wife's mind. "Calling him out would be an admission that you, my dear Hannette, were the first to break the vows you took before God."

Hannette, who faithfully attended church but was not much of a believer, was staggered. "You mean that you will not demand satisfaction?'.

"Precisely," he replied haughtily. "To preserve your honor, I'll forego demanding satisfaction."

For the first and last time in her life Hannette von Tenck burst into tears. Her husband was more than a hero, he was a saint! What he was proposing to do for her not a single man in Austria had ever done for any of her friends! Her fair name meant more to him than his own. She drenched his hands with her tears and, wracked with sobs, threw herself on his chest with a vigor that made him reel. She swore eternal, though not necessarily faithful, love.

"I'll be very careful . . ." she added, energetically blowing her nose. "You'll never catch me again."

Serge Olevitch magnanimously accepted the promise and forthwith ordered their carriage.

Young Aloysus von Schimmel waited all evening, first at Sacher's and later at home, for the messenger who never came. He complained about his disappointment the next morning, but no one in Vienna would believe him. The story of the boar was still fresh in everyone's memory, and nobody for an instant entertained the notion that Serge Olevitch, that fine upstanding man, would back off from dueling with this wispy young man.

Nothing was heard of the happy couple for a long time, since there was nothing to say about them. Hannette Olevitch continued her gallops through the woods, hunting man and deer with equal lust. Serge Olevitch had a special chambermaid with gentle dark eyes and a maternal instinct. He smoked cigars, drank port, and even sometimes, when he had drunk a bit too much of it, dared encounter his wife in bed.,

After a few happy years he was finally charged by a boar, trampled, and mangled. No one noticed that the wounds were on his back. The funeral oration, delivered by the bishop of Thuringe, spoke of his valor and intrepidity to a congregation as credulous as it was griefstricken.

"La Futura"

Leonora Guglielmo, known as "La Futura," was still, at the age of forty, one of the most beautiful women in Naples. The name "La Futura," which she had acquired twenty years earlier, was well chosen. For twenty years she had been a symbol of pleasure, gambling, money, sex, and other excesses of passion for the gilded nobility, the beautiful people of Naples. And for some time now, ever since the Austrian occupation, she also represented the future in the simplest meaning of this word. Thanks to her relationship with the police and the city authorities, and thanks to her new affair with the Austrian colonel responsible for maintaining order, Leonora had several times been able—in return for large sums of money—to cheat the firing squad and the gallows of a number of princes, dukes, and other minor aristocrats.

Count di Palermo, who on that evening stood before her, piling bags of gold onto her bed, was not worried in the least. His son Alessandro, who was to be executed in two days' time for having killed a miserable Viennese captain in a duel, would soon return to the castle of his ancestors. La Futura undertook to make this possible. To be sure, it was an expensive arrangement, but stupid and odious though the count thought Alessandro to be, he was, after all, his son. And so Count di Palermo forced himself to be pleasant to this self-assured hussy. She must have sensed his fury and been amused by it, for she smiled as she lined up the bags.

"They're all there," he said.

"Good," she replied. "But, tell me, what does he look like now, your Alessandro? I can't quite remember him."

The count winced, not because she had used the familiar form of address, but because he was miffed that, even in this disreputable dwelling, his son had made no impression.

"You see," La Futura went on, "I have to find someone to take his place at the execution. I'll send some fool in his stead by making him believe it's only a mock execution. At dawn, all corpses look alike," she added with a titter; "but there must be some resemblance to the original."

"Alessandro is tall and blond," the count said proudly.

Then he continued, in a subdued tone: "He has a scar across his face ... a nail mark," he added in response to La Futura's raised eyebrows.

She turned away and appeared to be listening to an unfamiliar sound coming from outside. But the streets were quiet. She asked her final question in a level tone.

"No other distinguishing marks?"

"Yes, the tip of his little finger is missing. I can count on you?"

"You can count on me," replied La Futura. "Count Alessandro di Palermo will be presumed dead by all Neapolitans the day after tomorrow."

Left alone, La Futura hesitated a moment, then strode toward the alcove door and opened it. A dwarf sidled into the room.

"Frederico," she said, "you remember the dimwit, poor Margarita's boy. He was missing a finger, wasn't he?"

"Yes," the dwarf replied.

Although his face was already horrible, he nonetheless managed a look of horror. La Futura appeared to brood for a moment, then, with an air of regret, shrugged her shoulders and took hold of the bags of gold, which she weighed in her hands one by one.

"Oh well, a pity," she said. "Margarita is dead now. You'll have to find me a tall, blond man, Frederico. Scratch his cheek and be sure he is missing a finger. I need him tomorrow night."

Gabriele Urbino came to. He felt a sharp pain in his finger as he tried desperately to remember how he could have hurt himself. He lay in a dark room with his hands tied behind his back. All he could remember of that afternoon when he had been fishing was an absurd, small, misshapen form stretched out on the grass next to him. He had turned around to look. And then, nothing.

The door opened and an arm holding a candle appeared. The arm was followed by the hideous head of a dwarf, and behind him, the face of the most beautiful woman Gabriele had ever seen. He automatically stood up and leaned his back against the wall. The dwarf freed his hands with one stroke of a knife. Gabriele noticed then that his hand was covered with a white bandage. He looked at it unbelievingly.

"What's your name?" the woman asked.

"Gabriele." And in spite of himself, he smiled. The woman had a low, musical voice. A voice like a violin, he thought. He wanted her to go on talking to him.

"Why are you smiling?" she asked. She was so intrigued, she looked twenty years younger.

"You have a voice like a violin," said Gabriele. "I have never heard a voice like it."

The dwarf laughed and so did the woman.

"Good Lord!" she said. "You've been beaten up, your finger cut, you're in prison, and all you have to say is that my voice sounds like a violin! You were born cheerful, my boy. . . ."

"True," admitted Gabriele. And he also laughed.

La Future thought him cheerful and handsome. He was far more handsome than that Alessandro, whom she now remembered very clearly. This boy's hair was a golden blond, shining and thick, not the dull, straw color of the Palermo boy's. His eyes were a bright blue, not a lackluster gray. Too bad, she thought, truly a pity.

"Listen," she said. "Do me a favor; I'll pay you well. Tomorrow, the son of Count di Palermo is to be shot . . . with blanks. Still, he's a nervous type and I need someone to take his place. . . ."

She talked on, pouring out lies with which to bait her trap, but for once she spoke haltingly, unconvincingly. She was not as smooth-tongued as usual. She was well aware of this and bothered by it. But when she had finished, the young man was still smiling. She became irritated.

"Well, will you do it? You're to slip into his

cell during the night, put on his clothes, follow the soldiers—"

"Of course I will. Anything you like. . . . I wasn't listening."

"You weren't listening!" she replied angrily.

But he interrupted. "All I could hear was the sound of your voice. May I have something to eat? I'm hungry."

La Futura hesitated, appeared to seek the dwarf's approval, then suddenly made up her mind.

"All right," she said. "You're going to have dinner with me. We'll have a good meal with wine, the likes of which you have never before drunk and never will again."

And indeed, that very evening, Gabriele had the best meal of his life, accompanied by the best Cypriot wine to be had in Italy. He drank a lot; so did she. They were in La Futura's untidy and sumptuous room, a small island of satins, silks, and warmth amid the crumbling plaster walls of an old house in one of the residential districts of Naples. Sitting in front of a wood fire, flames and wine lulling them, the young man and the woman were soon cheek to cheek, then mouth to mouth, until finally Gabriele learned what sexual pleasure really is. La Futura probably had never before taken so much trouble over a man, and doubtless she herself had never felt quite such bliss nor so much bitterness.

"La Futura"

Count Alessandro di Palermo was pacing up and down in his cell. The jailer had reassured him; everything was going according to plan; but it seemed to him that La Futura was keeping him waiting. There was, of course, no question of his dying, he, Alessandro, son of Count di Palermo, a future count himself. He was much too wealthy for that. Nonetheless, that hussy was keeping him waiting. He, Alessandro di Palermo, was being kept waiting at the whim of a harlot and a simpleton, the victim who was to take his place. The thought of the guns pointing at him sent a disagreeable shudder along his spine. Thank God he would not have to face that; in addition to his other shortcomings, he was a coward: he had killed the Austrian captain in his sleep. Even his father did not know that. Meantime, day was breaking and his thoughts were gloomy. When the cell door creaked open, he sprang up, an ugly look on his face.

La Futura, in the light of dawn, looked pale; so did the tall young man behind her. He had dark circles under his eyes as though he knew what awaited him. Alessandro wanted to laugh when he saw that large peasant standing so straight and seemingly proud of himself. Very soon nothing would remain of him except a bloody little heap on the courtyard pavement.

"You're late, La Futura!" he said furiously. "You've been well paid, haven't you?"

"Better late than never," she replied. "Take off your clothes," she said to the young man behind her.

And the two men began undressing. The young man took off his rough cotton shirt while Alessandro removed his lace shirt; the young man took off his coarse linen trousers, and Alessandro his leather boots and magnificent silk breeches. They were now very nearly naked, facing one another. La Futura's eyes went from the white, soft, skinny body of the Palermo son to the golden, slender, strong body of the peasant. Her stare was so eloquent that Alessandro saw it, understood, and exploded with fury.

"You dare compare me to that beggar!" he said. Blind with rage, he raised his hand at La Futura as if to slap her, not without pleasure, for he had always enjoyed hitting women. But before he could touch her, the peasant had thrown out his arm and struck him on the chin. Alessandro di Palermo fell back, hit his head on a beam, and was knocked unconscious. La Futura started toward him and stopped.

"What did you do?" she asked.

Gabriele, half-naked, immobile, looked like one of those statues of wrestlers imported by the Romans in olden times.

"He almost hit you," Gabriele said. "No one will ever hit you in front of me," he added reassuringly.

He took La Futura by the shoulders and enfolded her in his arms. With her face pressed against that naked shoulder, she could smell country air, sun, and, more penetrating and lingering, the odor of their recent lovemaking. She gently disengaged herself, turned away, and in a low voice said: "Get dressed." And as Gabriele reached for the lace shirt, she added in a harsher voice, "No, your own."

And so it was that at dawn in the month of May 1817, Count Alessandro di Palermo died abjectly, sobbing and screaming that he wasn't himself. As for La Futura, she was never again heard from. At least, not in Naples. It was rumored that she had been seen in Parma, dressed like a respectable woman, on the arm of a tall, blond man. But no one believed it.

A Country Outing

The summer of 1940 was a glorious one; blue sky and golden fields of wheat bordering the road were the unlikely setting for an unending stream of refugees. Trucks, sports cars, sedans, all bumper to bumper, proceeded at a speed regulated by Stukas as they plunged from the sky like vultures descending upon their prey.

There were not many Rolls-Royces in this motley column, and the one belonging to Madame Ernest Dureau, of Dureau Enterprises, was the occasional butt of gibes from other drivers who were not sorry to see that war does not respect social hierarchies, that some of the rich had had neither the time nor foresight to leave before they themselves had.

Hélène Dureau modestly lowered her eyes before those ironic looks, just as she had done only a month ago when, decked out in evening clothes and jewelry, she attended an Opera gala. The double row of onlookers had given her the same look, but there had been no trace of irony then. Hélène Dureau was of the Chevalier family, an accident of birth that had segregated her from the common herd.

Her young lover, Bruno, on the other hand, who was also in the Rolls and whose family circumstances were more modest (he came from the Pas-de-Calais) tended to put on airs, even on this summer's day, as if he were still at some exclusive Parisian party. There was something about him that seemed to proclaim, even in such circumstances: "Yes, I got away, I live with the rich and powerful." He obviously looked upon his status as gigolo as his crowning achievement.

Sitting next to Bruno was old Baroness de Poquincourt. Having miraculously found in her luggage an ebony rosary, which no one would have expected her either to have or to make use of, she fingered the beads and tearfully muttered endless and incomprehensible litanies. Her slack mouth, shining with lipstick that had become smeared by the heat, moved incessantly. From time to time her sucking noises got on Hélène and Bruno's nerves. A succession of calamities, missed trains, and mechanical breakdowns had brought this threesome together on the crowded route. Twice already it had seemed that the German planes were deliberately flying straight over the Rolls.

There seemed to be a bottleneck down the road, for they had been in the same place for almost an hour, in the full sun, exactly three meters away from the delicious shade of a plane tree; three meters in which were standing an old Rosengart, two bikes, and a handcart. Quite unconsciously Hélène Dureau's glance rested on the tan, blond nape of the neck of the young man with the cart. He leaned on the shafts, calmly smoking a cigarette. There was nothing in his stance to indicate he thought himself anywhere but in his own field. He was tall and neatly put together. Hélène hoped he would not turn around; she was sure he must be quite homely.

What a moment to speculate on a young man's looks, she thought and looked away, but not soon enough, for Bruno had followed her glance and was already sneering.

"You're sorry you're in the Rolls, my dear Hélène? You would prefer a more rustic means of transportation?"

His face, normally pale and too thin under a head of shiny black hair, had flushed. Anger had injected a tinge of vulgarity into his painstakingly refined voice. Bruno was a competent, relatively courteous lover, but he possessed the aggressiveness of the lowborn. Hélène, who occasionally remembered with delight dreadful scenes she had had with other lovers, always resented his occasional lapses from good humor.

"We're certainly lucky to have this Rolls," the old baroness said on a positive note. At least inside it we have some protection."

"Don't you believe it." said Bruno. "The merest bullet would go through it like paper."

The newly-pious baroness looked at him with an anguish bordering on despair. Hélène was surprised to see her lips quivering, lips ordinarily so firm and given to issuing orders. The old lady had been the arbiter of Parisian society for thirty years. She was shocked and dismayed to discover the Führer's Stukas did not accord her the deference to which she was accustomed.

"What on earth are we doing here?" she asked truculently. "It just isn't fair!"

And indeed, thought Hélène, for a woman who banned all political discussions in her house, who knew everything there was to know about surrealism and nothing about National Socialism, for a woman who had such charming German friends and who for five years had recited Heine at poetry gatherings, for a woman who had always worshiped at the altar of Wagner, this machine-gunning could be only a frightful mistake. She probably was persuaded, conjectured Hélène in amusement, that all she need to do would be to step out on the road and show her face to those naughty pilots—who were, alas! too far away to see—and they would disappear, beating their wings in apology.

A slight movement stirred the stream of traffic, and Hélène, sighing with relief, put back in her purse the wringing-wet handkerchief with which she had been mopping her face for the past half hour. Perhaps now they could drive along faster; a cool breeze might revive them. . . . But the chauffeur had barely put the car in gear when the droning started up again. The noise came from a distant black swarm that sounded inoffensive at first but soon became deafening as it turned into a snarling cry, like that of a tortured animal. Then, all at once, their fury unleashed, the Stukas dive-bombed the column of people and vehicles.

The planes came from far away, from Paris or Germany, and everybody automatically turned to look, everybody except Hélène, who had finally seen the young man's face. Contrary to her expectations, he was handsome, with a suntanned, open, carefree countenance. His good looks reassured her, for no good reason.

"Good Lord, it's starting again, there they are," the baroness's plaintive voice could be heard. She took up her rosary again with ring-laden fingers as Bruno involuntarily hunched his shoulders. The young man looked down for a moment; his eyes met Hélène's and, surprised, remained fixed on her. For one second, everybody except these two seemed turned to stone. All the others had fused into one being, possessed of one single pair of ears, awaiting in a hypnotic trance the ineluctable descent of the swarm. Somewhere, a child cried . . . then suddenly, regaining the use of their limbs, dozens of barely human creatures hurled themselves into ditches. The baroness had already opened the car door, completely forgetting that she was unable to do it without the help of her chauffeur. Bruno had gotten up and was pushing the baroness without even noticing the serene immobility of his mistress. The young man had smiled through the window that separated him from Hélène as if to an old acquaintance. Hélène could not help smiling back.

Bruno's voice, shouting from the ditch, woke her up. "What are you doing? You're crazy!"

She automatically turned toward him, as did the young man, and reluctantly the two of them went off simultaneously toward the same tree. Bruno cast a furtive, panicky, angry look at the young man, but fear proved stronger than jealousy and, as the air above them was rent with the ghastly sound of over-revved engines, this became the only reality; he put his head on the ground and his hands over his head. The baroness, in an unaccustomed pose flat on her stomach, revealed vaguely cubic contours and for a second Hélène smiled. She herself had stretched out, but on her side, leaning on

her elbow as though at the beach. She felt the burning sun through the leaves warming her cheek and
ear just as her eyes became riveted on one of the
planes that hovered over them, seemingly motionless, as if catching its breath before plunging. It was
small and black against a sky white with heat; presumptuous, ridiculous, rather like an expensive toy.
Like her, the young man was leaning on his elbow
a couple of meters away, his gaze equally fixed on
the airplane.

There was a momentary lull before the plane
detached itself from the others; then suddenly, as if
unable to resist the force of gravity, it plunged toward their tree. The sound made Hélène close her
eyes. She lifted her hand to her ear and all at once
the earth seemed to heave with nausea, a frenzied
rat-a-tat shredded the grass, sending bits of paint
flying over the magnificent, abandoned Rolls. Unable to bear the sight of that enormous, prehistoric
object, that metal monster bent on her destruction,
Hélène scrunched up and clung to the tree trunk.
As she hugged the rough wood she could feel the
warm bark under her fingers; she could not remember ever having loved anything as much as that tree.
With a long, whistling noise the plane was now
going up again, victorously flying into the sky while
cries, moans, calls rose all around them. From
where she was, Hélène, her eyes still shut, could
hear the shameless sobs of the baroness and the
chattering of Bruno's teeth. She guessed his face to

be as convulsed with fear as she had earlier seen it convulsed with rage. She knew the plane would come back; this was only a momentary respite.

Good Lord, she thought, perhaps I shall die between these two mean-spirited, absurd people. If I am wounded, they won't know how to help me; if I am to die, their faces won't help me pass over. . . . For a second she saw her past, present, and future: so lamentable, so bereft of warmth that her eyes filled with tears. She angrily wiped the tears away as she raised her head. She did not want the others to see her tears, for they would instantly assume they had been caused by fear; she did not want them, even in these final moments, to think that she was of their breed. And yet. . . .

"He's coming back! He's coming back!" the baroness shrieked.

Hélène saw the murderous robot up high, higher even than the last time. Someone within her, the overprotected little girl, began to whimper, to pray to a God she had long since forgotten. It would be unbearable to hear that deafening noise, the whining of the engines, again. Something else was going to happen to her, something almost worse: a fit of hysterics, panic, a mad dash onto the road that would bring her in the path of the bullets she wanted to escape. Just then a shadow came between her and the innocent rays of the sun as the blond young man knelt at her feet.

"It's strange the way it makes things shake," he

said. "You're not too scared?" He spoke under-standingly, with a confident sweetness of manner—as though he found the whole setup ridiculous, but acknowledging there was indeed something to be scared of. To be afraid to die, that was over-reacting . . . or so his expression implied.

"They're going to have their fun for another five minutes, then they'll take off," he said, sitting down and leaning his head against the tree trunk, "but your Rolls has had it."

He stood over her. Looking up, she saw him upside down. She could see his checked shirt open on a strong neck and the line of his well-defined jaw, which did not even quiver as the plane approached.

"This time they'll get us!" shrieked the baroness.

And indeed, the noise was worse than it had been at any time during the rout of the last two days. Hélène was nothing but the prey of this deafening noise, she was going to die, she was dead. And when the man fell on top of her she thought for a moment that this was the beginning of her burial. She felt the hard body shudder, and to stop herself from crying out, she put her mouth against his muscular arm, covered with blond hair.

He smells of grass, she thought hazily as she became aware of his heartbeat.

The airplane was now far away. She took her mouth off the unknown arm and moved her head a little. The body on top of hers also moved and fell on its side, thus pulling her out of the sheltering darkness in which she had been buried. The first thing she saw was a red stain, and stupidly she wondered where it had come from. Then she understood. The young man was stretched out next to her; he was very pale, his eyes closed. He had a wound at rib level, and blood was slowly oozing from it. Suddenly she realized that it was she who ought to have been wearing that scarlet flower if the handsome young peasant hadn't thrown himself on top of her.

"What's your name?" she whispered urgently. Suddenly it had become imperative that this man stay alive, that she know his name. Perhaps by calling him quietly, pleading with him, she could keep him on this earth.

"Quentin," he replied, opening his eyes and putting his hand on his wound.

"Are you all right?" came Bruno's voice from behind. It was so colorless and unfamiliar that she barely recognized it.

She did not answer but slipped her hand under Quentin's, on the open wound, squeezed her fingers without disgust into the warm blood so as to staunch its flow.

The farm smelled of mushrooms, a wood fire, and laundry. Gingerly perched on kitchen stools, Bruno and the baroness sulked. The walls of the overly large room were covered with posters of bicyclists and football players. Hélène and the young man's mother watched over his sleep. The bandage made a lump under the sheet, and from time to time one of the women checked to see if it remained unstained.

Far away, far, far away, a thousand kilometers away in Portugal, a large transatlantic liner lay in wait for them. They were to have boarded it; but ship, port, the America she knew so well, all seemed unreal to Hélène now. Life, real life, was in this room: the clucking of hens under the window, the burning silence of the countryside at three o'clock on a summer's afternoon. This was a silence she had never known before. She had no plans at all for the days to come, nor the slightest recollection of, what for four decades, had been an extremely full life. That life had ended under the tree amid the whining of airplanes. Absentmindedly, Hélène said to herself that she simply must change her jacket, the jacket on which the blood had now turned an ugly brown.

The woman sitting next to her had gotten up a second before she herself heard the wounded man's voice. Hélène admired the prescience of maternal instinct. The young man had raised himself on his elbow and was looking at them wonderingly; then, recognizing her, he asked with delight: "You're all right?"

Hélène smiled and nodded.

"Quentin, do you feel better?" his mother asked.

In a gesture of surprise, without taking his eyes off Hélène, he felt his wound. The sun's golden rays sawed the room in half, lighting up the dark wood of the bed and Quentin's naked torso. His chest was covered with blonde hair. Just like the arm, Hélène suddenly remembered, and to her surprise felt herself blush. How could she look sensually at a young man who had saved her life and who was now lying defenseless, as defenseless against shrapnel as against the kisses of a stranger?

"You'll stay for a while?" he asked, but so cheerfully that the question was more like a statement.

Baroness de Poquincourt was obviously getting nervous. She paced up and down the large kitchen and occasionally stumbled on the uneven tiles, spoiling the majesty of her celebrated walk. Bruno had stretched out his legs and laid the palms of his hands on his knees, in a position more suited to a club chair or bar stool than to a caned kitchen chair. To tell the truth, Bruno's cashmere clothing and the baroness's Carven coat had lost some of their elegance in this rustic décor. Hélène wondered if she herself didn't look like a ridiculous, displaced upper-class matron. For the first time in her life her fortune put her at a disadvantage. And yet, when her husband's business had required it, she had inaugurated countless nursing homes and hospitals, always on the arm of some prominent minister. Then, however, she had been a benefactress; now she was a beggar. Quentin's blood had flowed instead of hers. And although they were only a few hundred yards from the highway and could still hear the din of its traffic, she felt far, far away from her own world. There was no telephone on this farm, no butler to carry out her orders. The Rolls was probably still standing on the road with all of its useless, twisted chrome.

"I hope your savior is better," said Bruno sarcastically.

The baroness stopped her pacing, one foot in the air. She too looked resentful, rather like a female pheasant whose eggs had been stolen from under her. Hélène wanted to laugh. They both looked at her as though, deliberately and under shocking circumstances, she had just bolted with a gigolo. After all, I could have died, she said to herself, and the thought crossed her mind that they might perhaps have preferred to transport her corpse in the Rolls rather than do without that car. Did Bruno have any affection for her, or did he feel nothing more than gratification of his vanity, an appreciation of the numerous financial advantages he derived from their liaison? Did he find any charm in their lovemaking beyond that of fulfilling brilliantly his role as a male? He was a "good lover," as they said in Paris, but Hélène had never known exactly what that meant.

"How are we going to get under way again?"

asked the baroness, shifting her weight to both feet and making the change from a vacillating pose to a positive, assured one.

"The Rolls is wrecked," said Bruno. "There isn't a single car around. All these poor souls have scurried away like rabbits," he added with a splendid absence of self-consciousness (for, after all, what were they doing, the three of them?).

"And, believe me, when I tell you . . ." continued the baroness, whose rosary had disappeared in her jealously guarded green lizard purse. An isolated farm was, to her mind, just as dangerous as a sleazy cabaret. Nonetheless, the tile roof must have reassured her somewhat. Her voice shook with indignation as she went on: "There isn't a telephone within eight kilometers. I can't believe it."

"What good would a telephone be?" Hélène asked. "The lines would be down." She sat next to Bruno and turned instinctively toward the chimney, much as the usual inhabitants must have done.

"I've sent Edmond for news," said the baroness, starting to pace again, "but he made it plain that he would probably catch a train somewhere. We mustn't count on him. Anyway, Hélène, I've said this from the very start, your chauffeur does not inspire me with confidence. If only you had done as I suggested and taken Léa Carlivil's. . . ."

"Must we talk about Léa's chauffeur?" Hélène asked plaintively. "I don't know what to do. I can't ask. . . ."

A Country Outing

She stopped and made a gesture of helpless-ness. For once she couldn't ask her husband, Ernest Dureau, the efficient and positive Ernest Dureau—who for years had managed all the practical details of her daily life, and perhaps of her emotional life as well, or so she sometimes thought. There was a kind of brutality in his complaisance, attenuating his implied if equivocal generosity.

Quentin's mother was coming down the stairs. She looks like a very old woman, Hélène thought, but she's probably no more than forty or fifty. She was embarrassed to note the beady-eyed, pitiless stare of Baroness de Poquincourt as she took in the thick body, the wrinkled, leathery face, the shape-less garments of an indeterminate color. Actually, she must be my age, Hélène thought, and momen-tarily recoiled at the idea.

"My poor ladies, I don't quite see what you're going to do," said the woman. "The doctor said just now that there are no more trains running."

"But surely there's a hotel somewhere," said Bruno. "Even a little hotel with a telephone."

The woman looked at him with a mixture of surprise and amusement, for he had spoken with that imperious, affected, slightly shrill tone he used with headwaiters, and which, Hélène noticed for the first time, made him sound castrated and inso-lent. An unfortunate combination.

"You poor man," said the woman pityingly as she sat down beside them (to the shocked surprise of the baroness, who had quite forgotten that she was not in her own house on Avenue Henri-Martin). "You poor man, the nearest hotel around here is fifteen kilometers away, on the other side of Giens. And the owners closed it ten days ago. They even boarded it up." She started to laugh before adding, as if to explain: "They're Parisians." (The word "Parisians" seemed to imply cowardice.)

"We can't stay here," said the baroness, who had now placed her feet gracefully at right angles. This was her favorite stance for delivering fiats, as when she decreed that so-and-so simply couldn't be invited or such-and-such a play could not possibly be seen. It was the oddest feeling to observe the mechanics of such familiar mannerisms under these adverse circumstances. For the first time in ages, the teenager within Hélène came to life, an amused, highly critical, and facetious teenager.

"Well, you can't do anything just now," the woman said good-naturedly, "as long as the road's the way it is."

"You must be joking! We simply can't stay here!" The baroness sounded outraged, as if she had been invited to a public dance hall, as if the woman had asked to house such unsuitably dressed freaks, people who had nearly cost her her son's life. Hélène half-expected the baroness to add, "Please don't insist!" but for once she remained silent.

"I have two bedrooms upstairs," the woman continued in a level tone. "My oldest son's and the farmhand's; they're both in the army. They left me only Quentin for farm work. And the wheat hasn't been brought in," she added in a suddenly worried voice.

"I must confess I'm exhausted!" The baroness was very good at quick turnabouts. Her querulous voice became plaintive, the hand that held the purse became limp, and she dropped her chin—the picture of an elegant woman in distress. "I must lie down," she said, and she walked to the stairs. She even leaned on the arm of Quentin's mother, who had also risen, just the way she used to lean on the arm of the American Hospital nurse when she had one of her celebrated attacks of lumbago. Hélène followed while Bruno, looking nauseated, brought up the rear. The sun was going down. Through the window Hélène could see that the shadows of the plane trees were perceptibly lengthening in the fields.

Dozens of telegrams went off from the Giens telegraph office the following morning once Bruno, perched on an ancient bicycle, finally reached it. Baroness de Poquincourt, though revolted by her surroundings, had snored loudly all night in a farmhouse room devoid of the slightest comfort, while in the other room, Bruno, bitter and furious, had tried to quarrel with Hélène. Hélène, who normally snapped back when he was in one of these moods, had remained completely indifferent. She let him talk without even answering, only aggravating his exasperation.

The bicycle ride at dawn did nothing to reconcile him to his lot, and upon his return the farmer's wife, without so much as asking, handed him a pitchfork, accompanying the gesture with these peremptory, compelling few words: "Since Quentin is sick . . ." She led him to a field that had been harvested the day before. He felt caught in a nightmare. When he returned at about four in the afternoon, stiff and burned to a crisp by the sun, he detected a look of rebellion and compassion in the baroness's dark eyes—she was shelling peas, her hands encased in suede gloves—but in Hélène's gray eyes—she was manning the stove and shouting answers to the commonplace remarks Quentin issued from his bed—he thought he saw a look of unholy amusement. Her cheeks were rosy and, noted Bruno bitterly, she looked ten years younger. He had barely the strength to swallow some soup and a slice of much too salty ham before collapsing on his bed. The night before he had cursed it, but tonight it seemed the height of comfort. He slept so soundly that he never heard Hélène get up in the night, or whisper in the dark of the adjoining room, or moan in gentle pleasure at dawn just as the roosters were beginning to wake up the countryside.

Thanks to the great debacle of 1940, for three days each of the three exiles discovered and reacted to new experiences: the baroness to the charms of country living; Bruno to manual labor; Hélène to satisfying lovemaking.

With the help of the telegraph operator and a number of friendly contacts within the army of occupation, Ernest Dureau eventually succeeded in hiring a limousine that was to deliver the threesome safely to Lisbon. But order had not yet been completely established in France, communications were not always clear, and it was in all good faith that Lieutenant Wolfgang Schiller, a young pilot in the Luftwaffe, spotting a limousine in the forbidden zone, machine-gunned it thoroughly. When he soared away into the blue and gold sky of Touraine, there was no sign of life in the limousine.

The disappearance of these three people soon merged with other disappearances in the world of Paris music lovers. Ernest Dureau remarried in New York in 1942. Only Quentin felt a slight twinge for a few years whenever he saw a Rolls on Route 703. But he knew full well that the adventure had been nothing more than the result of circumstances and the whim of a rich woman.

Partway Round the Course

It was not until the twelfth hole that Cyril Double-street began to feel sick. The sun was beating down fiercely on the links of the Detroit Country Club, and Cyril, although burning hot, felt icy cold. Yet he was in good health; his conscientious doctor had recently assured him so. Actually, his only ailment was his age: fifty-five. He was breathing hard, which he found all the more irritating since neither Joyce nor David Bohen, her new young conquest, appeared to be in the least out of breath. Of course they were, respectively, twenty-eight and thirty-two years old. One must face the unwelcome fact that occasionally "the age of one's arteries," as he termed it, was frighteningly similar to one's actual age. Anyway, ever since the ninth hole young Bohen had been casting him furtive and smug looks, no doubt gauging how close he was to achieving his ambition: to shake off the old dog Cyril before the end of the round—to put him out of the running, once and for all, in the Joyce stakes. Had Cyril Doublestreet entertained even the slightest illusion about his chances of success when he had first courted her, he would certainly have had to admit they were nil this morning. But he had known for some time he hadn't a chance.

For five years now he had had no hope of getting beyond the first stages of a flirtation. He had given up any thought of success. It was quite a comedown from past performance, but now he was resigned to having become and remaining "that charming Cyril Doublestreet, who used to be so handsome." The past tense was the only one that could be applied to him without ridicule. The present and the future had lost their glow. No, he was not, nor would he ever be, Joyce's lover. Of course, young Bohen could not be aware of this firm, if involuntary, decision, but Cyril began to think the young man's ferocity shocking. All three had gone out the evening before, along with Sarah, a friend of Joyce's, and had not turned in until five o'clock this morning. There had been champagne, noise. Waking up at dawn had been rather painful. Cyril had not at all cared for the mocking tone of admiration the young man had adopted when he saw him arrive on time: "What? Already up? You really are wonderful!" Joyce had involuntarily shot him a look more compassionate than enthusiastic.

It was his turn. Smiling, Cyril raised his club and brought it down hard on the ball, which for an instant had looked like Bohen's head.

"Nice shot," Joyce said pleasantly as she turned toward him. He looked at her blonde hair, blue eyes, fresh red mouth, her slender, tanned body. He saw all this and felt himself withdrawing; his admiration for her was that of an aesthete, not of a man admiring a woman. Joyce must have sensed the withdrawal and seen the regret in his look, for she continued to smile and leaned against him with her hand on his shoulder. She had an infallible instinct and a warm heart; her youth was generous— unlike that of that little jerk David.

The latter had just made a superb shot and was already walking on. Cyril, whistling softly, followed. His legs shook, his heart thumped, and at the thirteenth hole he suddenly felt nauseated. As he raised his arm to hit the ball, he had a spell of dizziness. I'll never make it round the course, he suddenly thought, horrified. What excuse could he find? An urgent telephone call to be made—on a Saturday? No one would believe him; he had always been the idle, charming Cyril who, if he forgot an engagement, simply sent flowers the next day; who never forced himself to do anything he did not wish to do; and who, besides, had never allowed anything serious to interfere with his pleasures.

The golf course waved sickeningly before him for miles. He found the bright green grass blinding, and the jet-black hair of the handsome young man made him think of the angel of death. Obviously, he could hit his ball wide of the fairway, but he knew that the caddy would find it; in any case that would give him only a short breathing spell.

Cyril Doublestreet scanned the landscape, a hunted look in his eyes. The windows of the first house on the edge of the golf course shone three hundred yards away. He saw a woman open the window wide and lean out to breathe the morning air before disappearing inside. She had something pink around her head. It was a lovely shade of pink, and it was this delicate color that suggested the solution to his problem. His club slashed the air; the two young people cried out simultaneously: the ball, after a spectacular flight, had gone right into the open window.

"Good Lord!" said Cyril, "What an idiot. . . . I slipped. . . ."

Joyce laughed, and already the caddy was looking at him, but Cyril said in his most self-righteous tone: "I'd better go and apologize; it's the least I can do. Why don't you just go on without me?" He went down the slight incline, relieved. Whatever the reception accorded him, he would have ample time to pretend it had been a warm one. It would certainly allow him at least three quarters of an hour to catch up to his young companions.

"Should we wait for you?" shouted Bohen. Cyril smilingly waved no. Suddenly he felt invigorated, even curious to see the face under the pink scarf. Perhaps a ravishing woman? Perhaps the woman at the window would turn out to be as seductive and licentious as Maddy Christer, the woman of whom he had been reminded, the woman who loved that color. Perhaps she would offer him one of those long, pale, icy gin fizzes he had been thinking about for the past ten minutes?

He rang the doorbell of a house that looked like any other rich country house on the far outskirts of Detroit. Automatically he tucked in his shirt and smoothed his hair with his hand. The door opened and at first he could see little in the semidarkness. He heard the woman's voice before he saw her. Because it was so young, carefree and gay, it took him a moment to realize that this was the woman he had seen at the window. Probably the housekeeper.

"I bet this is yours," she said handing him his ball. "Do come in."

"My apologies," said Cyril as he crossed the threshold. "I came to see whether I had caused any damage."

He took a quick look behind him. In the dis-

FRANÇOISE SAGAN

tance, in the far distance now, the other two appeared to be turned toward him, but even if they
were not looking at him, they could still have seen
him. He quickly stepped in, determined to talk to
this woman for at least ten minutes.

"I hope I didn't break anything?"

"You did; a hideous vase. Come and see."

She preceded him up the stairs, humming.
They came into a bright room; he at once recognized the window and then he stopped, stricken, as
he saw the remains of what must indeed have been
a hideous vase.

"Oh dear," he said looking up, "I am truly
sorry."

It was then that he finally got a good look at the
woman's face. She must have been about forty-five;
she had dark hair, a smile full of humor, and a
serene, gentle face, or so it seemed to Cyril.

"How on earth did you drive it so far?" she
asked without a trace of animosity. "Balls usually
end up on the other side."

"I slipped . . ." Cyril began, then stopped.

He realized suddenly that he wanted to tell this
woman the truth. There was a tolerant, amused look
in her eyes, which made lying unnecessary, or
which at any rate had such an effect upon him.

"I was exhausted," he said. "All this green was
too much for me, and I didn't know how to get out
of the game. So I aimed at the window, and by
chance—"

Partway Round the Course

"Well, you might have killed me," she said with a laugh, not showing the least surprise. "Aren't you ashamed of yourself?" She sat down as she spoke, and with a purely social gesture invited Cyril to do the same. He accepted readily, with relief. If the people who own this house return, he thought, what a figure I'll cut: club in my hand, discussing my stroke with the maid.

She must have guessed what he was thinking because she began to laugh and to reassure him. "They're in Florida. I come once a week to air the place out. You were lucky. One day earlier or later you would have broken a window. Do you think the vase was valuable?"

"Oh no!" Cyril replied at once, picking up the pieces and turning them over in his hand. "You see, I collect antiques. Having said that," he concluded honestly, "it looks to have been so hideous that they may well have paid a good deal for it!"

She started to laugh and as she turned her head, the sun shone on her black hair and on her eyes, which were so light brown they were almost amber. A very pretty woman, Cyril thought; or one who once was. This was strange work for her. Had she been his housekeeper, he decided quickly and cheerfully, he would promptly have made her his mistress and set her up in a place of her own. He sat up straight and flashed his most seductive smile. He might well not be handsome, but he had had time in the past fifty years to realize that women liked him, and he knew how to appeal to them.

"What would you like me to do?" he asked. "Shall I leave you my card, my address, or a short note for these people? Good Lord! How ghastly!" he went on as he looked over the decor. And indeed, everything was imitation Chippendale, cheap oriental rugs, and bad reproductions.

"Would you like something to drink?" the woman asked so courteously that Cyril instinctively got up and, bowing slightly, introduced himself: "I beg your pardon, my name is Cyril Doublestreet. I ought to have started with that."

"My name is Mona," she said, also getting up and going to the back of the room. "What will you have? There must be some tomato juice left and perhaps some vodka."

"Do you think your employers would treat me to a drink for having broken their knick-knack?" Cyril asked with a laugh.

"Certainly not. They would have already called the police."

Cyril, following her into the kitchen, noticed the curve of her full hips, her strong neck, the impression of calm strength she conveyed. He realized, with a pleasure tinged with embarrassment, that this time he was looking at her not as an aesthete but as a male. Mona, with her pink scarf, tan blouse, and mules, was considerably more exciting than the beautiful, willowy, stylized Joyce.

Partway Round the Course

The house was partially closed, shaded and cool. Cyril felt his heart beat faster, but it was not like the thumping of earlier in the day. It was not the tempo of fatigue, but another tempo, a familiar one he thought he had forgotten.

She had a glass of grapefruit juice in her right hand and was still smiling. Her hip pressed against the sink and she looked at him with a warm and thoughtful expression.

Why was she smiling? Whom was she making fun of? Cyril wondered, perturbed. He took her suntanned hand in his. It was a strong hand, warm and full, a real woman's hand, a hand that was now closing over his while her smile grew slowly blurred as Cyril's face drew near to hers.

One hour later, Cyril Doublestreet caught up with his young friends at the club bar. They were sitting with the Nortons, Westwoods, and Crosbys, all of whom greeted him with glad cries.

"So, what did you do? What was the lady like?" Bohen asked jokingly, a mixture of condescension and disapproval in his voice.

"She must have been something to keep you so long," Joyce said somewhat sourly.

"Good old Cyril, always on the prowl," Crosby added with a leer.

Cyril said nothing as he sat down. To his surprise, the remarks annoyed him as much as if they had been undeserved. He remembered how, ever

FRANÇOISE SAGAN

since his early youth, he had boasted flippantly about his conquests. For the first time in his life he felt a little ashamed. How could he see Mona again tomorrow, laugh with her, if he allowed them to go on like this?

"The ball had fallen into the bathtub," he said with a smile. "I practically had to take apart the entire plumbing to get it out. Luckily the children helped," he added imprecisely.

Bohen snickered, Joyce looked away, and his friends, disappointed, went on with their gossip; he was no longer the man of the hour. But by leaning out a little he could see the window in the distance, and in the sunlight it appeared to be winking at him.

One Year Later

She placed her coat on the sofa and, although she knew she was one of the last to arrive, took the time to comb her hair, very slowly, in front of the vestibule mirror. She could hear the noise in the living room and could already single out Judith's neighing laugh, but she did not recognize any of the other voices.

This was the first time in a year that she would see him. She had no longer expected to do so, despite the likelihood of its happening. Judith had had to repeat twice the same little sentence: "You know, darling, I've asked Richard and his new wife; you don't mind, do you? It would be absurd now . . ." etc., etc."

She had replied: "Of course not; I'd be delighted. We parted the best of friends, you know. Of course I don't mind. On the contrary. . . ."

Only, Judith did not know to what extent that "on the contrary" was the palest reflection of truth. Had she been able to finish her sentence she would have said: "On the contrary, I haven't been alive since we stopped living together. On the contrary, my only hope of coming to life again someday depends entirely on him, on the impossibility that he'll ever again love me." But she could not say these things even to Judith, who was, after all, her best friend.

Everyone understood that the separation had been hard on her, and everyone knew how deeply she had been hurt. But one year of despair over a separation was the allotted maximum. It was taken for granted either that she had recovered or—and this was not put into so many words—that she must pretend she had. Besides, it was neither easy nor convenient for a Parisian hostess to invite a single woman; if, in addition, the single woman was given to melancholy, it became downright impossible.

After three months, Justine had realized that she must be cheerful if she did not wish to be forgotten, that she had no option but to pretend that she was passing effortlessly from the role of happy wife

One Year Later

to that of vivacious divorcée. The combined responsibilities and attributes of a couple had apparently devolved upon her: it was up to her to demonstrate the male's traditional independence and zest for living, i.e., his carefree attitude; and at the same time she was to manifest the female's meekness and gentleness, her trusting nature. And this was what Justine, who had once been a happy, loving, fulfilled wife, had endeavored to do day after day in order to stay afloat in the ocean of solitude into which Richard had cast her.

She thought she had succeeded. Bit by bit the smooth, rounded shape of her happiness had acquired angles. She herself had become sharper, brighter, bearing the weapons of a "liberated woman." She was probably the only one who knew and admitted, after sleepless nights spent in tears, that this liberation was nothing but despair. Nonetheless, she had worn the mask of a proud, modern young woman, the product of introspection and of a piecing together of what she had read and remembered. She had hidden behind this mask for one whole year now, and no one had thought to look behind it, to ask: "And you, Justine, how are you really?" Her family, her friends, her concierge, her boss all seemed to look with a new respect upon this elegant, self-sufficient Justine. Some men seemed to find a certain charm in this caricature of independence—or at least this was how Justine occasionally thought of herself.

Only tonight the problem was no longer to enlist the support of a group more than willing to provide it, but to show this mask to the man who had forced her to fashion it. The man who had compelled her to wear it so that she might repudiate him—rather like a reverse Pygmalion. The man who knew, and could not pretend otherwise, that there was a naked, raw, desperately familiar face somewhere under that mask. The man who would laugh at her pretense of independence and barely smile at her supposed gaiety. Richard. Richard, who had walked out on her right here in this very apartment one year ago.

She combed her hair even more slowly now. One year ago, the hair of the woman reflected in the mirror had been darker, less blonde. On that day she had worn a somewhat girlish, periwinkle blue dress, quite unlike the ravishing flame-colored suit she saw in the mirror today. That other woman had been paler, but with a fuller face; and her eyes, instead of being brilliant, dark, and carefully made up, as hers were this evening, had been filled with tears. That other woman, on that night one year ago, had most certainly not been silently combing her hair in front of a mirror. Instead she had hardly been able to see her face through the tears, her attention riveted on a cold voice beside her, a voice saying: "You simply must understand that this time it's final. And the reason I'm walking out on you in front of everyone, in this crude way, is so that they'll help convince you that it's really over.''

She took out her compact and listlessly powdered her nose. Actually, her makeup was perfect; she had worked hard enough on it before going out. It was for Richard that she had put it on. She had lengthened the oval of her eyes, emphasized the curve of her mouth, highlighted the shadows made by her cheekbones just the way Richard liked them, oh, a hundred years ago. She could pretend, of course, that she was doing it for Eric, for Laurent, or even for Bernard, but never, even for a second, had she tried to find in those three faces any reflection of her own. Their faces were not mirrors, they were blank windowpanes. This evening, at last, for the first time in days and nights that had been uniformly empty, she was going to see herself reflected in the eyes of someone else.

She went into the living room and did not, at first, see Richard. Judith sounded cheerful, animated, perhaps more animated than usual. Very soon Justine found herself face-to-face with the stranger, the "other woman" whom she still thought just as awful as she had originally. The "other woman" still had that snub profile, she still had that insolent voice, she still held her head at that same angle. Standing next to her, smiling gently in an avuncular way, was Richard—Richard's stand-in really, a tall, suntanned, elegant man with the voice,

FRANÇOISE SAGAN

eyebrows, and firm handshake that Richard used to have. Justine smiled at him hastily and moved on to another couple. She must have taken longer in the hall than she had realized, for already Judith was clapping her hands, shepherding her little group to the dining room.

They were thirteen, fourteen counting her; six couples more or less united, with Judith's ever-so-charming cousin and herself providing the dismal spectacle of celibacy.

She sat on the same side of the table as Richard, so she was unable to see either his face or his eyes. But opposite her sat his wife, the beautiful Pascale. Pascale, who had captivated the guests. Richard had certainly lost nothing in the exchange: Pascale dominated the conversation with entertaining observations and a ready, ferocious wit. A strand of black hair kept falling across her forehead, her eyes shone, her voice was becoming hoarse from laughter. She's pure charm, Justine thought with detachment while her own dinner companion paid her innocuous compliments she barely took in.

She felt curiously let down. This dinner party to which she had been looking forward for so many days, and which was to have been the highlight of the week; this party at which something was bound to happen, which had seemed to her to be fraught with danger but also to hold the possibility of poignant triumph, which was to have soared above uneventful days; this party had so far been thoroughly flat and showed every sign of remaining so. She would smilingly bandy a few words with Richard; the others would discreetly applaud their civility; then they would go home their separate ways and tomorrow Judith could tell her friends: "You know, I had Richard and Justine to dinner, and it went off extremely well! They were like two strangers. . . . Funny, isn't it?" Then perhaps Judith and her friends would make some bittersweet comment on the fragility of love. Suddenly, Justine yearned to have dinner over with; she wanted to skip coffee, cognac, the usual talk and routine compliments about the meal in the living room afterwards. The comedy was odious. Her uncomplaining acceptance of the situation did not for a moment alter the fact that the only man she had ever loved or ever would love, the man whose absence had for months plunged her into despair, the man who had transformed her life into a series of inconsequential happenings, that this man was here, a few feet away from her, still out of sight, as out of sight as he had been for the past year when he had been physically miles away. None of this would prevent her from going home alone, unhappy, beaten, just as she had done exactly one year ago. That she was not in tears tonight altered the situation not one whit.

After dinner, she told Judith she was going home early: "I'm tired; I have an important meeting in the morning." Judith listened absently; some of the couples in the living room and in the little room next to it were becoming noisy and, like a good hostess, she was keeping an eye on them. However, realizing there was something she ought to remember, she affectionately patted Justine's shoulder for a few seconds until it came back to her.

"And so," she finally said gaily, "you've seen Richard again. How long has it been? One year already! How do you think he looks? A little tired, don't you think?"

"A little," Justine replied between clenched teeth. But she did not believe one word of it. Richard was still as handsome, as seductive as ever. He was still the proud, unfaithful Richard to whom she was shackled by a tragic love entirely out of keeping with the atmosphere of this drawing-room comedy. She had indeed seen Richard again, and once again taken the measure of her defeat. That was all she could have told Judith—had Judith been interested. But, absorbed in her duties as hostess, she saw Justine as only one cog in the party wheel, a not entirely indispensable cog if Justine judged herself correctly. Without making other farewells, she set on her way unobtrusively.

Before going into the coatroom she stopped in the hall for a moment to pull up her shoe strap; when she stood up she had already heard the first sentence. It was uttered in the hoarse, gay, triumphant voice of a few moments ago, at dinner.

"Can't you understand that it's all over, really

over?" this voice was saying. "Don't force me to walk out on you in front of your friends. Do I have to make a formal announcement to them before you'll believe me? I don't love you anymore, Richard. This really is the end."

Then came a man's voice, breathless, pleading, almost unrecognizable, a voice that was not in the least like Richard's beautiful voice. Then words that she did not catch, perhaps even a blow, a cry. Then unhappy murmurs. She did not stir when the couple entered the living room through the other door. Justine shook herself, flew to the sofa, picked up her coat, and fled down the stairs.

Only in the cool air of the Boulevard Saint-Germain did she think to put it on. She carefully slipped it over her shoulders, one sleeve at a time, then meticulously buttoned it all the way down. She walked quickly to the taxi stand on the rue de Grenelle. A spring breeze blew on the boulevard and Justine, to her horror, hating herself for it, suddenly felt lighthearted.

The Distant Cousin

"Spas are bad enough when the weather is good, but rain brings on suicidal tendencies," said Charles-Henri de Val d'Embrun, thirteenth viscount of that name, talking out loud to himself as he counted for the sixth time that day the sum total of the louis d'or he had found in the turned-out pockets of the various items of clothing he had piled up in the middle of the room. Now he clutched thirty-eight of them in his hands. Thirty-eight miserable louis. All his life he had been accustomed to squandering them without a thought for the future; for some time now, however, he had been forced to make superhuman efforts to check their flow. At the end of the week a whole ten of them—ten even when converted into thalers—would be eaten up by the suite of rooms at Brenner's, the indispensable suite of rooms at Brenner's, the only "suitable" hotel in Baden-Baden. The only prey in sight, his only hope, was Fräulein Hettingen, the charming Brunehilde. Brunehilde was flanked, naturally enough, by Frau Hettingen, an imposing and formidable Munich matron who was herself accompanied, predictably, by a French friend, Madame de Cravelles. Charles-Henri, having made inquiries, learned that Madame de Cravelles was a distant cousin of Herr Hettingen—very distant, to judge from her graceful carriage and melancholy look.

The combination of these two females over forty—he himself was forty-three—led the viscount to believe his task an impossible one. Yet he must lead this wealthy young woman to the altar, even if he had to compromise her first. Only in this way would he preserve his good name and dishonorable way of life, both of which now stood in jeopardy.

Charles-Henri de Val d'Embrun, catching sight of himself in the mirror, saw there the reflection of a wretched, distraught man. Instinct and pride made him straighten up, square his shoulders, brush his moustache. He smiled as he saw his splendid teeth and was relieved at the transformation: once again he was the handsome, brilliant-looking young man he had stupidly persisted in remaining for the past twenty years.

Charles-Henri believed neither in work nor in its attendant virtues, nor even in plain old virtue itself: he believed only in the original Latin root, *virtu*, i.e., courage. Sometimes it seemed to him more courage had been required to keep up his revelries than would have been required to achieve virtue. Many a time some well-intentioned relative, grieved to see the waste of a good name, glowing health, and handsome physique had endeavored to restore all such by marrying him off to some not unattractive young lady of fortune and ancient lineage—a lady who would have been happy doing just that. It would have been well within his power to lead a pleasant, easy life with a wife, horses, liveried servants, and mistresses met at the Opera. But Charles-Henri had spurned all compromises. In a proud show of independence he had followed from city to city, from capital to capital, from bed to bed, all the women who in his eyes corresponded more or less to his concept of love. His fortune— or rather, his father's—had been swallowed up in this pursuit, which was why tonight he had to force himself to dream about Brunehilde Hettingen, heiress to the Munich house of Hettingen and Hofmeister, with capital amounting to one hundred thousand thalers.

The ladies took the waters at eleven in the morning, an hour at which Charles-Henri was still sound asleep, and again at four in the afternoon, the hour at which he had decided, two days before, to launch his campaign. His old friend the concierge had arranged a meeting through the kind services of a phony marquise. After the introductions, Charles-Henri had gone into his inconsolable-brokenhearted-but-willing-to-be-comforted act. Young Brunehilde had devoted herself to the task, achieving a certain success despite her quite remarkable clumsiness. The mother took longer to respond, but she finally succumbed at dessert with the help of violins and whipped cream; she began reminiscing about the romantic charms of Bavaria in the sixties, before she had made the acquaintance of Wilhelm Hettingen. With the aid of his wit and his château in Dordogne, and with these ladies plunged as they were in hope and remembrance respectively, Charles-Henri might well have been successful that very evening—had it not been for the distant cousin, who had plainly earned that adjective "distant" for more than kinship alone. She observed with a coldness oddly tinged with approbation the encircling maneuvers of the hapless viscount; he had even caught her nodding admiringly when he alluded to the ducal crown of his cousin Edmond, then cleverly let fall the extent of his acreage in the Dordogne.

Oddly enough her approval cramped his style rather than encouraging him. First of all, the two Teutons were altogether too blonde, their flesh too pink, their eyes too blue. The cousin had black hair, so black it was almost blue. It was his favorite hair color, and, despite the lines around her gray eyes, they sparkled with a bold gaiety of bygone days, a gaiety he considered out of place in view of the heartbreaking account he had been giving of his life. She looked both aloof and amused, a state of mind with which he was familiar and which could only be the result of a background of solid wealth and a life spent making the most of it—i.e., gratifying one's pleasures. He and she probably both belonged to the same world. But she at least, he thought grudgingly, had been able to provide for herself. It was even possible she was the one who held the German purse strings, at least if one went by her air of calm assurance or the respectful attention the other two paid her. "Marie suggests this. . . . Marie thinks that. . . . Marie would like. . . ." They seemed to talk chiefly about her, about *her* wishes. If he were to succeed at all, thought Charles-Henri, then his marriage, too, would have to become one of her wishes.

Seated one day on the terrace of Brenner's in his white linen suit, his hand resting on his Malacca cane, a brandy and water in front of him; sitting there penniless but elegant, nonchalant, and haughty, Charles-Henri de Val d'Embrun began to think that he would have to come out into the open with Madame de Cravelles. He would have to admit that he was a ne'er-do-well, though a contrite one, or about to be a contrite one. He would lay his cards on the table.

Or ought he to continue with his lachrymose act, which he was finding harder and harder to keep up?

He was so absorbed in his own thoughts that he paid no attention to the elderly couple who had just issued from the casino, rather like Orpheus issuing from the underworld, and collapsed on the chairs behind his. They were haggard and pale, mumbling under their breath.

He had run into this couple, who were world-famous and deserved to be, in all the casino cities he had frequented. They were old-guard Russians who, in ten years, had managed to liquidate their immense family fortune bit by bit, estate by estate, verst by verst. Despite their efforts—fate is sometimes cruel enough to smile upon the most willing victims—it was said that they still retained palaces in Moscow and St. Petersburg. Totally enslaved by their passion, they had survived into this century without seeing any part of it. All that was known about them, except for this shared passion, was the disordered lives they led and their extravagant generosity. Their path was strewn with poor devils hoping for handouts. Only their gambling whims and extreme mobility allowed them to escape these hangers-on.

Charles-Henri looked at the couple with a mixture of revulsion and compassion, much as one looks at the handicapped, but he was so wrapped up in his own schemes and uncertainties that he probably would have heard no part of their conversation had not one name, repeated over and over again by the old gentleman and his wife, finally penetrated his consciousness. It was the same name he had been hearing for several days from his "fiancée" and her mother: *Marie.* The coincidence made him perk up and listen.

"We'll have to do something about Marie before we leave," the man was saying. "She looks awfully pale to me this season. . . ."

"Souvaroff hadn't a penny," the woman answered. "Yet Marie knew that. She kept Nicolai's children for three months before taking the job reading to that Englishwoman, and now—"

"And now it's worse than ever," the man went on sadly. "Can you imagine teaching manners to those fat women! You know, don't you, that the mother pretends she's a cousin: Germans adore titles. If she only knew that right now Cravelles is doing hard labor in Guyana. . . . Yes, we'll have to leave Marie something." And he shouted for vodka so loudly that everyone on the terrace looked around, everyone except Charles-Henri de Val d'Embrun, who remained frozen.

Five minutes later the ladies appeared. With the viscount as escort, they proceeded to the kiosk to hear the concert. The selection was by Massenet. The two blonde ladies wiped tears away in time to the music. The viscount, unusually pensive and worried-looking, gratefully accepted Cousin Marie's suggestion that they not meet again until that evening at eleven at the casino ball. He put the ladies into a hackney carriage with his customary courtliness but, to the deep disappointment of young Brunehilde, did not squeeze her hand as he had been doing for the past two days. In fact, he'd forgotten, so put out was he by the sight of the two German ladies reclining comfortably on the carriage seat while leaving their "distant cousin" to perch on the jump seat facing them. Worse, it was on her he kept his eyes fixed as the carriage drew away, and to her he waved. She smiled back and looked suddenly ten years younger, as Brunehilde was able to ascertain when she turned around, for the carriage was heading into the sun and the light shone full on Madame de Cravelles's face. Conversation was strained during the return trip: the two ladies, all at once mindful of expenses, could not help acrimoniously mentioning the price of the room occupied by the Frenchwoman.

"What do you advise I do?"

Marie de Cravelles's answer was to drop his arm and give a half-joyous little laugh hardly in keeping with the anguished tone of her escort. It was past midnight. The Baden-Baden casino was lit with a thousand lights and the crowd was waltzing energetically in the summer night.

"I advise you to waltz with Fräulein Hettingen instead of with me. But first, I should like you to get me an orangeade. I'm dying of thirst."

She was wearing a beautiful dress of pale gray lace that brought out the sea-green color in her eyes and enhanced her slenderness. Charles-Henri wondered how he could ever have paid attention to any other woman. But for once I must have kept my eye on the main chance, he thought to himself, with premature and cynical self-satisfaction. He followed Marie along the garden paths toward a buffet festooned with flowers and now almost deserted. When he saw her take her glass, empty it all at once, her head thrown back, thirsty, cheerful, carefree— everything he loved in life—his self-satisfaction vanished. Heaven help us, he said to himself. We may belong to the same world, but we're both in the soup.

He made her sit on a wooden stool under a trellis and, leaning toward her, said with a purposeful look: "I have something important to discuss with you; it's of vital importance to me."

"I know, I know," she replied, trying not to laugh. "You are Viscount Charles-Henri de Val d'Embrun, life has been unkind, you've given your heart only to women who haven't any, and you want to settle down in a Christian manner on your estate in Dordogne. Isn't that it?"

"You exaggerate," Charles-Henri protested weakly, involuntarily blushing with shame. "I didn't say that precisely. "You're overstating the case."

"Am I? You surprise me. . . . I thought I heard the cry of a wounded, honorable man."

"Please, Cousin Cravelles . . ." (Charles-Henri had decided to plunge) ". . . please. . . . Have you heard from Cousin Wilhelm? Is business in Munich good?"

She stopped laughing and they looked at one another for a moment in silence. Suddenly Marie looked over forty again, and her dress was not new.

"Yes, thank goodness," she replied calmly. "Yes, thank goodness, business is good. We both need that, don't we?"

It was Charles-Henri's turn to look away, and with a nervous gesture he pointed to the worn-out spot on his shirt front. Without thinking, she raised her hand and put his jacket back in place—a gesture, they both realized simultaneously, that turned her into an accomplice. They looked into each other's eyes, smiling tenderly. And indeed, there is nothing more to say, thought Charles-Henri wearily but with some happiness. Her simple gesture had summed it all up: his little acts and her seeing through them, the help she was immediately prepared to give him. For the first time in ages Charles-Henri felt faint stirrings of emotion. He struggled feebly.

"Let's suppose that my wooing of that nubile,

The Distant Cousin

overfed mare is successful. You'll lose your job. How long have you been teaching these ladies how to live? Or at least trying to?

"Six months," she said, making a face. "And you, how did you find out about me?"

"It was the Russians. The two gamblers. You know them, don't you?"

"Oh yes! Varvara and Igor. They're darlings. They always talk too loudly, wherever they are."

She smiled tenderly, without a trace of resentment. Charles-Henri liked that.

He thought hard. "How did you know about me?"

"Oh," she said, her head thrown back as she laughed (once again she looked twenty), "that's easy. I have never yet met a single handsome man who in twenty years' time has known only heartless women. That isn't possible. Your tactics are based on an absurdity, my dear Viscount. You'll have to change your story."

They both laughed so heartily that young Brunehilde, who was waltzing a few feet away with an uhlan in the same weight class as her own, shot them a furious look, totally lost on them in their dark corner.

"You haven't answered my question. What would you have done?" Charles-Henri pursued doggedly, without noticing that he had slipped into the conditional tense. "What would you have done if I had married your pupil?"

"Oh, my first reaction would have been a sigh

of relief. And then, honestly, I don't know. I'd have cursed you and at the same time pitied you. But tell me, that estate in Dordogne, is that also imaginary?"

"Certainly not," said Charles-Henri in a belated rush toward respectability. "It really is in Dordogne. That is, far from Paris. The land's been heavily mortgaged for a long time and I've never been able to sell it."

"You were thinking of taking Brunehilde there?" she asked, unconsciously speaking in the past tense.

"Oh no!" Charles-Henri went on with an exaggerated firmness resulting from apprehension. "No, actually I've never known a woman with whom I wanted to live there. There, or anywhere else," he added. "I've never lived anywhere except Paris. I couldn't. . . ." He stopped in the middle of his sentence, tried to continue with it, then gave up. Those violins spelled danger; and so did his accomplice, with her sea-green eyes and carefree laugh, her face reflecting tender and extravagant memories, this woman with a past marked by apparently generous follies. He drew back when she put her hand on his and, anticipating her question before she had asked it, he shook his head.

"But why not? I adore the country!" Her smile, which had started in her eyes, had become irresistible, springing as it did from confidence, relief, and gaiety.

Charles-Henri resisted the smile with great difficulty and might well have missed his chance for happiness had not young Brunehilde chosen this moment to appear. Standing squarely in front of their table and seemingly carved out of the same hard wood, her eyes flashing, her voice loud, she said in French that was correct, at least grammatically: "My cousin seems to have forgotten her age tonight."

With dismay, Charles-Henri saw the smile vanish from Marie's face; he saw her hurriedly stand up, incline her head slightly and acknowledge her guilty and reprehensible behavior. He noted that she was about to apologize and realized all at once that he couldn't bear to see her do it in front of him, her natural protector and future lover.

"And I think you have forgotten yours," he said, getting up. "Your youth is no excuse, Fräulein Hettingen," he said with mock deference, "for forgetting ours, Madame de Cravelles's and mine; nor is it an excuse to absolve you from making your apologies. I am waiting." And he continued in this vein, even invoking the soul of his ancestor, Emery d'Embrun, who had spent five years in the Bastille for his insolence to Louis XIV.

The young Valkyrie, knowing nothing about such heroic precedents, hesitated, shifting her weight ungracefully from one foot to the other. Just like a bear cub, Charles-Henri noted absentmindedly. He did not dare look at Marie, though he yearned to take her in his arms as quickly as possible now that someone within him had made the decision for him, someone to whom he, Charles-Henri, had hitherto turned a deaf ear and who, perhaps, was nothing but a country squire, enjoying life, mindful of appearances, faithful to his wife, and quick-tempered.

"Mama . . ." the young woman began, "Mama'd say. . . ." She then stopped, her face suddenly red, and almost shouted, "I apologize," before charging off at an impetuous gallop.

Charles-Henri could have sworn that even the glassware shook and indeed his own laughter was echoed by the laughter behind him, laughter that stopped only once he had taken the distant cousin in his arms.

The Exchange

As England basked in a gentle autumnal sun, the massive and solemn towers of Fontroy Castle cast their lengthening shadows on lawns that were still apple-green. A horde of visitors, talking volubly, walked toward the rear gate supervised by tired but alert guards. It was almost six o'clock and the castle would soon be closed to these intruders. There was only one little group still tramping along the great hall. Because the guide was hurrying, worried and embarrassed as always when their lordships were in residence, he did not see the young scamp Arthur Scotfield disappear behind a suit of armor.

FRANÇOISE SAGAN

Scotfield was a slender, red-headed young man with an attractive, cheerful face who wore his threadbare clothes with laudable elegance. Right now, as he panted a bit in his hiding place, he congratulated himself. The small Franz Hals painting was right where he had been told it would be, at the end of the corridor, opposite the large paneled door. All he had to do was return when night fell, take it down, and make for the nearest exit. He felt as though he had walked for miles in this damned castle and wondered what manner of madmen could still be living in it.

Lord Fontroy relit his cigar for the third time. His complexion, usually brick-red, was practically purple tonight, and his wife, the still beautiful Faye Fontroy, shot him a half-worried, half-amused look. The dinner had been interminable and, really, their guest, Byron, ought to have known better than to arrive like this, the day before the hunt. His passion for her was no excuse for his ill-timed presence— more than ill-timed, in view of the filthy mood into which jealousy had plunged Geoffrey. Lord Fontroy had always been jealous—often justifiably so—and even now when she was well over forty (over fifty, her best friends said), he could not help darting his bloodshot eyes at any good-looking man who hovered in the vicinity of his wife. Angrily he stubbed out his cigar in an ashtray. Byron, sensing danger, unfolded his lanky Scottish frame and coughed lightly.

"Will you excuse me if I retire?" he asked in his high-pitched voice, which was what had kept Faye from paying much attention to him so far). "I think we're making an early start in the morning?"

"Right. At five o'clock," Geoffrey snapped.

Byron bowed to Faye and to her husband and went regretfully toward the great staircase. Faye, who had followed him automatically with her eyes, was startled when Geoffrey addressed her.

"I suppose you like him also."

"Come on, my dear, you've had a tiring day with that mob; their clattering footsteps could be heard in all the corridors. Haven't you had enough for one day?" she asked.

"That mob helps pay for your hats and your travels," Geoffrey reminded her bitterly. "My ancestors are stared at by clods every Thursday just so your whims can be satisfied. And now that wimp Byron comes here to stay under my roof so that he can make eyes at you. Dammit!" he shouted, slapping the arm of his chair, "I won't have you carrying on under my own roof!"

"Oh, come off it," said Faye soothingly. "Stop your beastly talk, Geoffrey. It's time to go to sleep." She got up. Lord Fontroy, despite his corpulence, followed her quickly into the hall. When, after an interminable walk, they finally reached her door, she turned and looked wide-eyed at her husband. "Would you like to search my room, Geoffrey?"

She felt like laughing but at the same time had

a nagging thought there was something odd about the wall behind Geoffrey, an empty space. She was sure there was something missing, but what? She started to ask Geoffrey but he grabbed her arm and pushed her into her apartment.

"You must forgive me," he said, "but I intend to sleep peacefully tonight. I'll unlock your door when I leave for the hunt with Byron, at five." He closed the door behind her. She heard the tumbler turn, not without squeaking, three times.

Her private apartments consisted of a huge, gloomy walk-in closet and a stately Gothic bedroom, the sole charm of which was the view, a delightfully wild one of the hills of Sussex. This was not the first time Geoffrey had locked her in like this, but she couldn't help laughing because this time it was quite unnecessary. She undressed, put on a favorite silk nightgown, and started to brush her hair in front of the mirror. Her hair was still red despite the passage of time. She looked at her gleaming teeth, her fresh, English complexion, her strong, slender body. She smiled at herself. Suddenly she stopped, her hairbrush in midair. She had just remembered what it was that had disappeared from the corridor: the little Franz Hals. She was sure of it. One of the tourists must have picked it up as he went by! She did not see how he could have left the castle with it, not under the butler's eye, the ever-watchful Gordon. Oh well, she thought, it's not much of a loss, and her smile grew broader.

The Exchange

The curtains in her room were being blown by the wind, and she realized she was cold. Where on earth had she put that delightful mohair blanket, a present from that delightful Edmond Brindeshoux? Was it Edmond or Pierino? She could not remember. The blanket was so light that it might have been made of swan's down. It must have been put away in the wardrobe at the back of the room, the one she seldom used. She walked quickly to it.

Opening the door, she found herself face-to-face with Arthur Scotfield. He literally fell into her arms, nearly suffocating from having been squeezed between a mound of slipcovers and the door. He sneezed violently four or five times from the moth crystals. What rotten luck, he thought—alarmed by a guard, he had sought shelter in what was probably the only occupied room in the castle. And why had this woman chosen *this* particular wardrobe, from among at least twenty others? She would surely start to screech and he would have to run down unknown corridors and certainly get himself nabbed by the guard. This was Arthur's sixth burglary, and the first five had been so successful that he felt this unfair. As he sneezed, he waited for the inevitable rumpus, but his sneezing stopped suddenly when he heard a cheerful, even amused voice say, "God bless you!" He automatically responded with a "thank you" and looked up.

He found himself standing in front of the beautiful Lady Fontroy, pictures of whom he had enjoyed looking at hundreds of times in any number of magazines. Now he found himself admiring those bare shoulders and tawny hair. This was the last straw. On top of everything else, he had to stumble upon the lady of the house! Even if she had not seen the painting, which he had buried under two slipcovers as if by reflex, she was nonetheless going to call her husband and have him thrashed. How was he to account for his presence? What could he use as a pretext for being here, at this time of night, in this room? His agile mind darted about wildly.

"Have you caught cold?" Faye asked kindly. "These corridors are terrible" As he did not reply, she shrugged her shoulders and smiled at him. "There's a fire in the next room," she said. "Come and warm up."

Staggered by her calm acceptance of the situation, Arthur followed her to the huge fireplace and sat down gingerly on the bench to which she pointed. The flames were high; they made large shadows that danced on the distant ceiling and cast a rosy glow on Faye's cheeks. She looked very young like this, and very vulnerable, despite her composure. What self-possession, Arthur thought admiringly; for, after all, if he hadn't been a gentleman he might have been a murderer and wrung her pretty neck. He gave her a reassuring and protective smile, which made him singularly attractive.

His clothes hang well on him, Faye thought,

The Exchange

and he could be very handsome in spite of his thinness. . . . His eyes and teeth are magnificent.

They looked each other over for a minute or so, then began speaking simultaneously.

"I wanted to tell you—" Arthur began.

"What are you doing here?" Faye asked.

They both stopped, surprised and embarrassed, then started to laugh. Faye spoke first.

"I said, young man, what are you doing in my room at this time of night?" she asked calmly.

And then the answer, the only possible answer, came effortlessly to Arthur. "I love you," he said. "I've often seen you at the races, in newspapers, everywhere. I've dreamed about you so often that I've risked everything to meet you. I had to see you and tell you." He was regaining his self-confidence now; he knew he had quite a line and a great many women had fallen for it. Furthermore, he had no difficulty in speaking of love. This Lady Fontroy was not in her first youth, true, but she was certainly seductive. He became even more eloquent. "Your beauty, the way you walk, the color of your hair, your eyes. . . . Ah! I never thought I'd get here. . . ."

She sat motionless, looking at him, then smiled affectionately, as though to an old friend and not at all as if she had just come upon him buried in her closet.

"It's very nice of you to have come all this way. I'm very touched. But you're a young man, a very young man, and I'm too old for you. You must forget me and leave as quickly as possible before they find you here."

Arthur nodded, vastly relieved but a little disappointed. However, he had been extraordinarily lucky that this woman was so matter-of-fact. He would leave the painting where it was and return, free, to London and explain to his partner that the deal had fizzled. There would be no trouble. Still, he would have liked to stay a little longer by the fire, opposite this exquisite creature. "Can't I stay a little longer?" he pleaded.

She shook her head and got up purposefully. "No, it would be taking silly chances."

He too got up, and saw her stop suddenly, frozen. She clutched her forehead. She was standing in front of the fireplace; in the light from the flames, he could see her body under the transparent silk, and his mouth felt dry.

"Good Lord!" she said, for the first time showing some nervousness. "You can't get out. Geoffrey, my husband, has locked me in until tomorrow."

"Locked you in!" he exclaimed, shocked.

"Yes," she replied, apparently not seeing him, her eyes fixed on the door. "Yes, my husband is jealous. He won't open my door until five o'clock tomorrow morning on his way to the hunt. How tiresome," she went on, sitting down again on the bench. "How tiresome, all those keys and locks.

What an obsession! Try the door anyway," she went on imperiously. "You never can tell!"

Arthur went to the door but, despite his skill with locks, he realized that this medieval contraption would not yield. She was standing behind him; he could smell her perfume and, in spite of himself, was thankful for Lord Fontroy's jealousy and the solidity of that lock. "I can't budge it," he said, standing up and turning to face her.

"Heavens!" she murmured, "what am I going to do with you until tomorrow?"

Their eyes met as they stood very close together; he felt slightly dizzy.

"I can't spend the night with a young man in love with me," she murmured dreamily. "It would be most improper."

But the word "improper" was smothered by Arthur's mouth on hers. He held her close, kissing her shoulders; he was slender and young and ardent. This young man smelled of sun, of old tweed, and she let herself lean against him, her eyes closed, a little smile on her lips.

At five o'clock the next morning, Lord Fontroy unlocked his wife's door as he went by, silently, he hoped, a little ashamed of himself. Byron was waiting for him below, shivering in the early morning. Lord Fontroy clapped him on the shoulders, almost affectionately, as he joined him. They strode off into the woods. As he checked his gun, he hoped he had not awakened Faye. He need not have worried; he could not have roused her—for the very good reason that she had not slept.

Young Arthur Scotfield lay next to her, naked and loving. The fire had died in the fireplace and dawn was breaking behind the curtains.

"You must leave now," she said in a tired voice, "and you must not come back. Take the second staircase to the right after the French doors."

He sat up in bed and looked at her. He had dark circles under his eyes and she herself must have looked frightful.

"I spent a marvelous night," he said in a very young voice.

She stretched out her arms, drew him to her, and kissed him gently on the corner of his mouth. "There, that's our farewell. Take your clothes, get dressed where I found you, and go quickly."

He did as he was told, backed out into the other room, and dressed quickly. Through the wardrobe door, which had been left open, he saw the small painting amid the slipcovers, and he hesitated. It would be too stupid not to take it, he thought. After all, she had said to him at one point that she did not give a rap for the castle, its furnishings, its valuables; that she liked only men and animals. She would not even see it. So he picked up the picture and started for the door.

"Arthur!" called a voice from the next room.

The Exchange

He stopped, put the picture on the floor before going back in. Faye Fontroy was sitting up, a pad of paper in her hand. She tore off a sheet, put it in an envelope that she sealed, and handed it to him. "Here you are, Arthur. This is a little note for you, a token of my affection. Read it on the train."

Touched, he leaned down, kissed the beautiful bare shoulders once more, and left quickly, picking up his loot as he went out.

Lady Fontroy's handwriting was large and generous, but legible. Seated in the train, Arthur read the letter, which said:

"Be careful, my darling. The painting is just about as authentic as your passion for me. (I too, from time to time, run low on funds.) It was a lovely night. Are we even?"

It was signed "Faye" and, after his initial astonishment, Arthur Scotfield began to laugh a clear, delighted laughter that made his placid fellow passengers look up.

A Question of Timing

She had turned on the TV and was looking at it from the sofa, where she sat with her knees folded under her, her eyes half-closed, in a position he had once described as her "feline pose" and which he now thought affected and mannered. She wore a white sweater made of very soft-looking white wool from which emerged her long, graceful white neck. Soft tendrils of blonde hair at the nape of her neck fanned out into a profusion of golden locks framing a ravishingly beautiful face. He had once quivered with tenderness as he contemplated her swanlike neck, her doelike eyes. At the height of his infatuation he had even attributed the gracefulness of that neck and head, the narrowness of her wrists, to fine breeding. Love had prompted him to use terms more usually employed by vulgar people. He had thought of his mistress as being "aristocratic" and, without finding the description laughable or commonplace, he had shown her the excessive care normally reserved for fine crystal or expensive flowers. Indeed, he had behaved like a flunky with social pretensions and he was now mortified because he realized he had loved a perfect object, not a real woman. He had loved his mistress as one loves money or art: aesthetically. And he was annoyed with himself for having used pretentious, paltry little words to describe an untrammeled, raw feeling totally unconcerned with respectability; for having wanted to giftwrap that fragile, wounded thing that love is. He had loved her discretion, her lack of mean reflexes, of pettiness or low instincts. He had loved her for what she avoided, what she was incapable of doing, for the protective barriers with which she surrounded herself. And yet what other love than a wild love did he consider to be real? He would a thousand times have preferred loving her for her infidelities, her stupidity, or some idiotic vice! In this way at least he could have understood both his misfortune and his luck and have been able to laugh at himself! Furthermore, he might then have known how to make the break tonight.

A Question of Timing

She stretched. She had on tapered black slacks that outlined her gorgeous body. There also he had been deceived, as much by himself as by her, because at night it was as if he held in his arms a fury, a slave, a bacchante, and he marveled at seeing her re-emerge in the morning, gracious and withdrawn. "Fire under the ice," he had said to himself. How could his love have progressed in such clichés? How could he have been sent into raptures by this ostentatious duality, and even have found it exciting? What real duality is there in a woman who is aloof in the daytime and passionate at night? Who, in both instances, behaves like a stranger, as much in her exaggerated reserve as in her excessive ardor? And yet he had enjoyed, he had thought it (horrors!) the most subtle of pleasures, to act out with and for her the part of a man of the world in the daytime and of a gigolo at night. Never, ever, had she treated him as an equal. A person in love does not make a show of gross disdain for the loved one, nor does that person inflict sexual deviations on the loved one. Their relationship was false, odiously false! And although no erotic recollection troubled his conscience, there were certain words uttered at parting—"See you soon, my dear"—spoken in indecently discreet tones, in front of friends well aware of their relationship, that made him blush. Into what shameful abyss, into what farce had he stumbled under pretense of playing a witty drawing-room comedy? How could he—who had loved and been loved, who still believed in love—have allowed it to become such a crude, shabby caricature?

"And what would you like to drink?" she asked in her best high-society manner as she looked up at him.

"I'll help myself. What about you?" he replied, ignoring her bogus refinement.

As soon as he'd spoken he felt ridiculous. No, it would be better to remain formal, to use formality as a shield for an elegant, cool, disdainful retreat. How does one decently leave a woman in whose warmth one has buried oneself for two years? Better to withdraw gracefully.

She neither reacted nor replied. He poured himself a drink with a steady hand, put back the shaker, which no longer seemed to belong on a shelf that had itself become unfamiliar. He then went over to an armchair that might have been a Louis XVI. He felt so lost in this house, in this little universe, every corner of which he had once known and loved, that he was almost relieved to see on the little TV screen the hypocritical face of a well-known politician. This time he viewed the face with a sort of sympathy, even contrition. "When I think that I used to think you ridiculous—self-important, pretentious, dishonest!" he said to himself, "when I think how poor in spirit and heartless you seemed, how frightened and vulgar under all that arrogance! Ha! I ought to have admired you. You're just like her."

A Question of Timing

He stretched out his legs and put his hands on the arms of the chair. He was resting. His body still that of a small boy asleep, a body still intact—this body would stretch out alone in a few hours, between two fresh, smooth sheets. After the end of the affair, of course, after the destruction of something that had never had any reality.

"It's crazy, isn't it?" she asked. "They all say the same thing."

He nodded. Once more he agreed. He always agreed with her. She spoke with such indifference, such derision, that it would have been pointless to contradict her, for she herself seemed always ready to give up whatever stand she had taken. But, in fact, she never really did; she clung to her prejudices, her personal experiences, to a code of living that had been culled more from guidebooks than from the Bible. And her weary voice, which dragged a little and was so convincing, was a cover-up for a frightened and thus pitiless woman. Yes, she was afraid: afraid she wouldn't have enough money, though she had plenty; afraid of being old, though she was young; afraid she would give herself away, though there was nothing at all under that air of elegance and offhand manner. There was nothing at all behind that facade, no haunting memory. Perhaps a man snatched from a close friend, or a show of greed, or one or two people wounded to the heart . . . at the very worst, orgies at the Trocadero or cheating at gin rummy.

FRANÇOISE SAGAN

And after he had left her, after the initial moment of anger and hurt pride, it would be fear that she would feel until she had replaced him: the fear of being alone, as though she weren't already so, forever so; as though it were not inevitable that she should die in solitude and terror, just as she had lived; as though her first cry when she had come into the world had been anything but the ferocious and sharp scream of a self-centered newborn babe. He suddenly realized that she was one of those women who are hard to imagine as children, and he now remembered that all the stories she had told him of her childhood—stories that were supposed to conjure up gardens, lawns, distinguished uncles, and tennis rackets—of that delightfully English and peaceful past, had always left him with the impression that it could all be reduced to a succession of raucous, cacophonous sounds, that in fact she had been attempting to transform into a fairyland a world filled with boredom, arrogance, and onanism. She was one of those people whose childhood seems murky, whose old age will be obscene. He even recalled how surprised he had been when she had told him about her first lover. He had attributed his astonishment to his mistress's fragility, to her air of innocence and chastity. He had realized that it was because in some obscure way she had remained in his eyes, in some mysterious meander of her innermost self, a virgin (despite her nocturnal excesses)—or else that she had never been one.

A Question of Timing

"What are your plans for tonight?" she asked.

He was tempted to answer tersely, "Walk out on you," just to see the change in the peaceful, smiling, and already approving expression on that beautiful face. And indeed, had he suggested going to the theater, to a beach, or making love, she would predictably have agreed. She would even have approved of his choice, would have led him to believe that, however odd, it was precisely what she had been wishing all afternoon. She would even have convinced him later that the play, the beach or seashore, the rumpled sheets had been her idea, that all he had done was to follow her lead. It was the same whenever he was funny, talkative, lively throughout the evening. She would take full part in the general laughter, but as they went home she would say to him indulgently: "You had a good time, didn't you?" This was her way of letting it be understood that the pleasant evening was a present from her to him. She wasn't a bit funny; she laughed when others were funny; she applauded intelligent remarks made by others, and cried out when she was being made love to well. But she herself never made anyone laugh, or think, and if one had pleasure in bed with her it was really only because of the physical mechanics of human bodies that made pleasure inevitable. Suddenly he thought of himself as one of those heavy, clumsy reptiles in an exotic quagmire who carry on their heads the kind of noisy, deadly, voracious, brightly colored bird that feeds exclusively on the waste and mud picked up by its carriers. She would easily find another crocodile or hippopotamus on which to perch. Because her plumage was so beautiful and her voice so compelling, no animal would be wary of her incessant and avid pecking. . . .

"I don't feel like going out," he said as he reached into his pocket for cigarettes. She smiled and with a quick gesture threw him a small, excessively slim, expensive lighter—a recent present from him. He caught it on the fly and was not at all surprised to find how cold it was, as though it had not been held in a human hand. It was as if gold and silver no longer acted as conductors of heat or desire when they came into contact with that elegant, cold, bloodless hand. Her lighter, her sofa, her house, her belongings, even her body—he did not find it disturbing that, although he had paid for all this, it did not confer ownership upon him. His only regret was that he had once cherished it all.

On the screen a man and woman were embracing. They were beautiful, as actors must be, and the woman's hand on the nape of the man's neck seemed full of tenderness, gratitude. There was something akin to madness in the gesture, something poignantly precious for which he suddenly, achingly yearned, to the point of dizziness. There was a lump in his throat, constricting his jugular

A Question of Timing

vein, impeding the flow of blood to his heart, preventing it from beating. He was alone, poverty-stricken, cold, afraid, and hungry; he was ageless, nameless, with no future, no friends. He was exposed and shivered with tenderness because on the screen a stereotype of an actress was kissing a very ordinary young actor. He had only to utter three words to the woman sitting there, near him, and she would take off her clothes, run her hands over his body, feel him, arouse him, say ghastly things, all of them lies, even say "I love you" and nibble on his neck. Afterwards the shivering would turn into teeth-chattering, which he would be just barely able to control, and he would be even more alone.

He looked at her. She was staring at the couple making love, her smile tinged with scorn, a smile that implied it was all really a pity, but after all that's the way love is.

He wondered in a sudden panic, if she does indeed scorn love, why does she continue to make love, to talk about it? By what right does she make use of its expressions, gestures, even put on its heart-rending mask? Suddenly he wanted to strike her as one might strike a forger. She had never loved anyone before him; she had told him so, and he had taken an idiotic pride in it at the time. By what imbecilic and criminal fatuity had he managed to hide from himself the inevitable corollary of that confession: that if she had never loved anyone before him, she would never love anyone after him, and furthermore had not really loved anyone in between. He had met her when she was someone else's mistress and had been delighted at the ease with which she had walked out on the other man for him. He had ascribed her ruthlessness to love, had attributed her readiness to his own charm, had viewed as impetuousness what was actually desertion. That was it; she was a deserter who went from one desert to another, in the process making everything around her arid, icy, and colorless: eyelashes, faces, carpeting, even the dawn. The other man had later killed himself driving into a plane tree. He remembered breaking the news to her gently.

He had a theory, nebulously formulated and perhaps foolish, but nonetheless a theory that guided him: one cannot be wholly involved with someone else without leaving an imprint of oneself on that other human being. Yet, she had not turned a hair when she had heard the news of his death. She had shrugged her shoulders slightly and turned away—from a sense of decency, he had thought. She had even said something about bad luck, and as far as she was concerned it must certainly have had all the earmarks of bad luck to have the man on whom she had walked out lose control of his car a little later. In no way did she consider herself involved in this man's life—so short a one. She had had nothing to do with this story of a love nor with that fatal accident.

Suddenly he shivered at the thought that it might not really have been an accident and that he himself might be slated for a quick death as soon as he left her. "The Third Fate," he said to himself, and by an ironic twist she reached out just then for the finely textured, multicolored needlepoint she had recently started. He saw her frown before methodically moving her long, tapered fingers. That useless bit of tapestry was symbolic and would remain so. It was inconceivable that she could knit a sweater, a hat, a bag, anything, for anyone else. He had never seen her pass the bread, nor hold a door, nor offer a light. And when she had tossed the lighter across the room to him a little while back, it had been done ostentatiously, so as to remind him that it was her present —an expensive one that, being in love with her at the time, he had bought at a jeweler's—that she was willing to lend him. She would never have given him something for nothing, and the only advantage he had, in her eyes, over the millions of destitute was that he could afford to buy her a meal at Maxim's.

Her eyes were lowered on her needlepoint, her brow furrowed. She appeared to be struggling with some technical difficulty. She set aside her needle, gathered her skeins of wool and, with a resigned look, placed everything in front of her.

How blonde she is, incredibly blonde, he

thought just as she turned toward him and opened her mouth to speak.

"You know, Thomas," she said. "He loves me. I'm going to leave you."

Suddenly he was stabbed with a monstrous grief; he wanted to vomit, to cling to her. And for one last time her blonde hair lit up his future life like a flame, and he saw what that life would be: hell.

Tears in
the Red Wine

One hour . . . I'm giving him one hour. That's the
longest any self-respecting woman will wait for a
man. At least a woman like me, a happily married,
beautiful woman, an acknowledged beauty who is
desirable, desired. A woman dozens of men are
running after. I can name at least six. A woman
wearing a ravishing hat and a beautiful fur piece,
who has been waiting on a stone bench in a square
in Paris for a man who is late. This is unbearable,
outrageous. I am beautiful, elegant, desired, and
absurd. Yet in one and a half hours I'll still be here,
waiting. I'll trample on my hideous hat and I'll leave

these stinking furs on this bench. And yet, when he comes, if he wants me to I'll take off my clothes right here in this square. I'll follow him on foot all through the city.

And if he doesn't come, I'll kill myself. I'll go home, kiss Henri, put my hat on the bed (since this brings bad luck), put my furs on a hanger (since I'm tidy by nature). Then, I'll take out the bottle I've hidden behind my makeup removers in my exquisite bathroom, I'll empty it into my hand, and I'll swallow with tepid water the bitter white tablets, one by one. Just the right number, not too many, not too few. I am not going to allow myself to be ridiculed by muffing my suicide. I've had enough ridicule. I love ridiculously, I live ridiculously, but I shall die with no comic overtones. I have no sense of humor left. Love, yes, with a capital L, but my sense of humor has long since flown out the window. Ever since Bernard Faroux.

Bernard Faroux! What a name! It has no charm, nothing. When I think that I was Roberta Durieut, a happily married woman, elegant, desirable, desired, etc. A woman who did not know Bernard Faroux. And for six months now I've been the wreck who does know Bernard Faroux, an insurance man who is neither particularly handsome nor intelligent, who is pretentious, selfish, and a boor who has been keeping me waiting for ten minutes—and whom I love. I won't wait one second more than an hour. Anyway, it's getting dark, this bench is ice-cold, the square is deserted. Anything might happen to me. I could be attacked, for example, by that bum who is coming this way with his bag, his hungry look, his filth. He isn't even old; he could easily wring my neck. What is he doing? How dare he sit on my bench? That's the last straw! What a picture we must present, me in my furs, he in his rags! That should make Bernard snicker. If he comes.

Lucas Dudevent, better known as "Lulu the Bag," carefully stretched his legs and sighed contentedly. He was right, except for the broad and her pelts, the bench was unoccupied. It was hell nowadays trying to find an empty bench. As soon as the weather improved, the carless citizenry swarmed over Lucas's benches, the lovely, smooth benches that were all his during the winter months. They lolled about inconsiderately on them for hours, mooching, reading books, sometimes—and this was the worst—keeping an eye on noisy brats who shot him dirty looks. But now it was night and this dark square, this hard stone bench did not appeal to the overfed and underfed types. Except for the brunette. Quite a looker, under that hat. She kept scanning the walk. She was obviously waiting for someone. You'd have to be a real stinker to keep a woman like that waiting.

If Lucas had not long ago given up beautiful women, beautiful cars, and our beautiful civilization, he would have made a pass at her. And if he hadn't been dressed the way he was, he might have done very well. Back in the sixties, when he was in his thirties, the handsome, well-dressed, and happy-go-lucky Lucas could have had anyone he wanted.

He opened up his bag, took out the bottle that was filled to the top, pulled out the cork, crooked his elbow, then stopped in midair. The shoulders of the woman next to him were shaking with silent but violent sobs, awful to behold. Lucas, in spite of himself, offered her his precious bottle. The glass made a clinking sound on the stone; the woman turned and Lucas saw her face-to-face. He noted the two pale eyes shining under the veil, eyes outlined with mascara and grief, eyes brimming with round, irrepressible tears. The two looked at one another for a long moment. Sad blue eyes, compassionate black eyes. Then she seemed to come to, murmured "thanks," and took a long pull on the bottle before giving it back to him. Her tears dried up instantly, her color came back, and she almost smiled. Lucas made note once again of the boundless benefits conferred by red wine.

"Helps, doesn't it?" he asked with the pride of a faithful consumer.

"It certainly does!" she replied, pulling a handkerchief out of her pocket. She blew her nose so vigorously that even she was startled by the noise. She looked apologetically at Lucas, who had taken his turn at the bottle and, ever the gentleman, showed no sign of hearing anything except the

Tears in the Red Wine

lovely melody of the wine as it coursed down his gullet.

"What kind is it?" she asked.

"Don't know," Lucas answered, wiping his mouth on his sleeve. "I do know it's thirteen percent. I get it at Dobert's. A pal. Want some more?" he suggested politely but without enthusiasm, for he had been counting on the bottle to last him all evening.

"No, no. Thank you very much," the brunette declined tactfully. "It really braced me. I needed it. . . ."

Since she herself had brought it up, Lucas felt justified in inquiring further.

"Depressed, or stood up?"

"I think I've been stood up. I've been waiting half an hour already.

"Must be a bastard," Lucas stated positively. "A real bastard, if you'll excuse me—"

"But I won't wait more than one hour," she said in a steady voice. "I swore it. At one minute to six I'm getting up. I'm going home. That's it."

"If I were you, I'd . . . oh well. . . ." He made a vague gesture, his face took on a thoughtful look, and he became almost handsome, Roberta thought.

"If you were I?" she took him up.

"It's none of my business, but I've waited for women on benches in the past and every time I waited more than one and a quarter hours, it ended up badly. Badly for me, that is. . . ."

She looked at him fixedly. "And the other times? When you left sooner?"

"When I left sooner, it was because I was able to," Lucas replied, looking at her in his turn. "They caught on and followed me."

There was a thoughtful silence. Roberta and Lucas seemed a classical pair: philosopher and pupil. She looked down at her feet, then up the path. Absentmindedly she put out her hand and Lucas resignedly placed the bottle in it. He was, after all, responsible for a fellow creature. She took a swallow—a long one, he noted sorrowfully—and wiped her mouth on her expensive sleeve with the same gesture as his.

"And when they had caught up with you?" she asked hesitantly.

"By that time I was home," Lucas said, laughing in spite of himself (his three front teeth were missing and it embarrassed him to let his new conquest see this), "and at home, there was Clopinette, who loves me," he finished briefly. Then . . ." He made a vague gesture that so clearly meant "then, out of the cold, under my bridge, with Clopinette . . ." that Roberta was filled with the same thought: then, out of the cold, at home in Paul Doumer Avenue, with Henri. . . .

She got up suddenly, dusted herself off. What a magnificent woman, Lucas thought, well dressed and everything.

"That's what I'm going to do; I'm going home."

"It hasn't been a whole hour, has it?" Lucas asked, his eyes crinkled up with laughter. He felt happy, like a practical joker. He was going to stay and see the guy. He looked forward to such a satisfying moment. Making a woman with eyes like that cry! He's not going to get away with that!

"I know," she replied, also laughing. "No, it hasn't been an hour. Too bad, I—good-bye, Monsieur. Thank you for the . . . thank you for everything." She made a gesture toward Lucas that encompassed the bottle (causing Lucas a brief moment of alarm); but already she was leaning over, putting her two warm hands on Lucas's; she gave them a little squeeze, then left quickly. She disappeared down the walk just in time, Lucas thought as he observed three seconds later, the arrival of a young man who was impatient, and fidgeted for the next half hour.

Just as it would never have occurred to him to apologize for his lateness, it would never have occurred to Bernard that Roberta might not wait for him; it was Roberta who should have been on the bench, not that debilitated bum who was laughing to himself.

But Roberta never again waited for him anywhere. Heaven knows why, Roberta did not love him anymore.

Incidental Music

The tune had come to him toward the end of the evening and he had found it so irresistible that for once he had taken refuge in the cloakroom in order to jot down the first measures in his little address book: *do-mi-si, si-la-sol.* . . . At first he had thought of it as piano music, but the first notes were so cheery, so free that he decided they needed an accompaniment. He undid his shoelaces, humming softly, and for a moment forgot the scene that Anita had begun in the car. But not for long.

"Are you listening to me? I'm not asking if you hear me but if you are listening to me." Anita was turned toward her husband, wearing an expression she thought was half-sad, half-sarcastic. Not for an instant did she imagine that her nose could be shiny or that her first wrinkles were cruelly outlined in the summer dawn; an unfortunate lack of imagination —though "lack" wasn't really the right word since, if anything, her imagination was excessive, though in one direction only.

Like a bird building its nest, Anita accumulated insignificant incidents bit by bit: isolated, even contradictory moments, which she miraculously succeeded in adding together. She would then, one fine day, triumphantly produce her accounts, the examples and proofs of her theories—theories revealing Louis's superficiality, indifference, snobbishness.

"But I am listening," he said weakly. Perhaps what he really needed was a jazz tempo: first a bass, a clarinet, perhaps a banjo. . . .

"I don't understand! I simply do not understand. I may be stupid—"

There are some possibilities that ought not to be explored, was the thought that coursed rapidly and gaily through Louis's mind, but he immediately put on a wooden expression, aloof, almost irritated. The mere supposition that Anita could be stupid: it was absurd, it obtruded, like some spoonerism, in a serious conversation.

"I don't understand either," he said. "It was a party like any other. . . ."

She neighed triumphantly and deliberately sat down facing him, her hands flat on the arms of the chair, her eyes gleaming with determination. It was, alas, a gleam that meant this was not just a momentary mood, one that he could change; they were in for one of those interminable arguments. He sighed and lit a cigarette as he wiggled his liberated toes with relief.

"You said it yourself, my poor Louis, 'a party like any other.' Neither better nor worse. A lost evening. What on earth can those snobs do for you?"

It was true that, ever since he had been awarded an Oscar in Hollywood the year before for the best movie score, a segment of Parisian society had made much of him. It was also true that he derived a childish pleasure from breathing the atmosphere of luxury, friendliness, and flattery that had been sadly lacking for so many years in his life —in *their* lives, he silently amended, for Anita had complained enough about their way of life during what she referred to as "the lean years." Her now blatant scorn for what she had once avidly wanted seemed a bit sudden and contrived. She was pretty, well-dressed, and obviously enjoying herself. What waspishness was the source of this increasingly pronounced contempt, Louis wondered.

She went on: "Do you know, for example,

what that beautiful friend of yours, Laura Knoll, said to me? Guess!"

'I'll never guess," he said firmly.

"I should hope not. She had the gall to say to me, 'How I envy you, dear little Anita.' " (She tried to imitate Laura Knoll but succeeded only in speaking in a strident, affected voice, quite unlike Laura's pleasant one.) " 'How I envy you . . . not your Louis's present success, but the difficult years. It must be wonderful to live with a creative genius! Money problems . . . bah!' "

Anita had uttered the last sentence with a blighting sarcasm that made Louis want to suggest to her that Laura's words were not far off the mark. Those difficult years, those lean years, had been the fulfilling, rich years of their love. For five years he had been madly in love with Anita, completely in her thrall. And if the prosperous years had coincided with the fading of his passion, that was not really his fault. He had brought his success to her; he had placed it triumphantly, stupidly perhaps, at her feet; and she could easily have made of it a shared success. Unfortunately, at just that juncture a joyless, arrogant intellectual had surfaced in her, a new woman whom he had not known nor had intended to marry. He no longer even wanted to tell her so; his only concern now was how to get away from her.

She kept on insisting, hammering home the point: "You aren't appalled? The callousness of that wealthy bitch, envying us our poverty? That doesn't shock you? Oh, but I'm forgetting: in this house Laura Knoll is a sacred subject."

"What are you getting at?" he asked, looking away nervously. For once she had struck home. He liked Laura, in spite of her minks; he hoped that soon, with a little luck, he would become Laura's lover. She had smiled at him a certain way during the evening; it had been a tender smile, reflected in her violet eyes, that would have been encouraging to a man even less presuming than he. He smiled. For two or three years now there had been more and more opportunities in that field but, even the three or four times he had taken advantage of them, he had done so with so much circumspection that Anita's allusions were gratuitous. He shrugged innocently, got up, stretched, and started for the bathroom. Anita's voice was still pursuing him as he stopped before his reflection in the mirror, the reflection of a thirty-five-year-old man who seemed a trifle tired, gone a little soft, but who still looked quite nice.

"I'm probably irritating you," the voice in the bedroom said, "but if I don't tell you the truth, who will? You need . . ."

And so on, and so on, he thought as he turned on the faucets noisily. *Do-mi-sol, do-mi-re.* Yes, there was a certain charm in that little air, an irrepressible gaiety that would even allow him to write it in the minor key and add violins without losing any of its

liveliness. Yes, he would need a large orchestra
. . . and he would ask Jean-Pierre to orchestrate it
. . . with rapid rhythms.

He took a tube of toothpaste, opened it, and
stopped dead. In the mirror he saw Anita's face
behind him, white with anger, convulsed with fury.
For a fleeting moment he wondered who this stranger was, this harpy who dared come between him
and his music. She took a couple of steps forward,
put her ringed finger on the faucet, and violently
shut it off. He saw the white hand redden at the
joints and noticed the fiery sapphire blue of the ring
he had given her two months before as a tenth-
wedding-anniversary present. They had married
"for better, for worse" without knowing (or at least
he did not know) that the better automatically en-
tailed the worse.

"You could at least look at me for once when
I'm speaking seriously."

She stood next to him, leaning on the wash
basin; her breathing was labored. They saw each
other in the mirror as two enemies; or, to be accu-
rate, she looked at him as she would an enemy and
he felt embarrassed, almost frightened by the feeling of hatred so close to him. Relax, he thought,
relax. He put out his hand, turned the faucet slowly
so that it would not splash, and carefully, perhaps
too carefully, put his toothbrush under it.

"It isn't a matter of 'for once,' " he said gently,
too gently. "You never stop speaking seriously.
Couldn't you just speak pleasantly?"

Incidental Music

She opened her mouth to protest, but he was already going on in an urgent, hurried voice that stopped her.

"Listen, we must stop this. You've simply got to stop criticizing me. You've got to change your attitude. You're exhausting me, Anita; you're getting in my way. A tune is running through my head right now, one I've been hearing for the past two hours. I hear it with a clarinet, a violin, a harp—and whatever you may say, however loudly you yell, this tune drowns out your voice. Do you understand?"

He was beginning to feel carried away by excitement, an excitement he knew to be dangerous but which he was powerless to stem. It was swollen like a river by dozens of little waterfalls, dozens of repressed bursts of anger. "And if that piece of music is good, I'll pay the rent with it, pay for the car, your dresses, my suits, daily expenses, even dinners in restaurants for all those people you have no right to despise. And, if necessary, I'll also pay for airplane tickets that will take me far away from you more and more often. And if need be, this tune will also pay the rent on another place and buy another car so that we can both lead separate lives, so that I can have the peace at night to hum a tune when I brush my teeth."

In the mirror he saw his wife flush, take a step back; he even saw the tears form in her eyes just before she turned her back on him and left the bathroom. He put the toothbrush in his mouth and started to brush his teeth carefully while his heart

FRANÇOISE SAGAN

thumped. He hated being unpleasant. Already he could foresee with resignation, a resignation mingled with pity and bitterness, the false and inevitable reconciliation in bed that would follow.

He bruised his gum and saw with indifference a thread of blood trickle down to his lower lip. To his surprise, the somewhat haggard stranger opposite him suddenly began to smile. *Do-mi-sol, fa-mi-sol* . . . there, he had found it! The tune really needed an organ. Not the murky organ of Catholic weddings, but the great vibrating organ of freedom. He must present the motif all at once, with no frills, perhaps with the help of an organ trumpet stop. He went back to the bedroom, humming, his step sure like a victor's—but victor of what a mean little battle, he thought as he saw on the battlefield his sad victim, clothed in a nightgown and dignity that were equally transparent. In order to assure her an honorable defeat he still had to touch her, and so he bent over this woman, resigned to sex.

Anita had been frightened, had shown it, and was undoubtedly annoyed with herself now that he was lying beside her. Doubly transparent, she also probably thought (as though their lovemaking had been a victory for him). He felt her growing nervous in the dark. He was trying to breathe regularly, deeply, the way one is supposed to when asleep; but this forced regularity was oddly suffocating to him. He was simultaneously smothering a cough and a desire to smoke as wild as his desire to laugh because Anita's face, a moment before, had been the perfect and comical example of pride defeated by desire. Her body, after an initial instinctive recoil, had so quickly sought his that they had bumped hard into each other in the dark and he had been on the verge of asking her what the trouble was before realizing what her movements meant. It was only the thought of Laura that ultimately made it possible for him to perform adequately as she sighed and groaned with pleasure. Nonetheless he continued to breathe with a metronomelike regularity. Very soon, he thought, he would be able to turn toward the wall with impunity, stupidly grunting like a male deep in restorative and inviolate sleep. He was already bracing himself to turn when Anita's voice stopped him. His breathing, shallow now, betrayed his wakefulness.

"How could we have come to this?" Anita's voice asked in a dull, sad tone—like the voice of that beautiful actress in *Hiroshima, Mon Amour,* was his irrelevant thought. He remained silent, cherishing one last hope, but the same, sad, gentle voice was already going on:

"Don't pretend to be asleep, my poor darling. Answer me. How could we have come to this?"

In spite of himself he heard his own voice reply: "Where? Come to where?"

"Saying the horrible things we've said to one another."

FRANÇOISE SAGAN

"What do you mean?" Louis asked, relieved. He had been afraid for a moment that she was referring to their recent activity, but luckily for Anita (as for most women) the desire of the male was in itself a proof of love—the very manifestation of that desire seeming to assure its passionate nature. "What do you mean? We've been stupid, got all charged up; it's nothing serious," he said reassuringly. "Now go to sleep."

"Not serious? Do you really believe what you're saying?"

No, he did not believe what he was saying, but he no longer felt like confiding anything to her; he would rather confide in Laura, or Bob, his best friend, or his mother, or the concierge—in anyone but her. He did not feel like discussing anything with her, and especially not the one subject she was really entitled to demand that he talk over with her and her alone, i.e. the subject of their future.

It really has become an impossible situation, he thought as she raised herself and, leaning on her elbow, looked down at the inanimate black mass formed, in the early morning light, by his shoulders and head. He could smell her fine perfume mingled with the odor of her body, of their bodies after their lovemaking, the odor that for him had once been the very odor of happiness, of a burning and tender love. Just then a panicky hand, a relic of the past, gripped his throat, shook out of it a dry sob, a tearless spasm, the violence of which astonished him. I ought to speak to her, he thought quickly, and just as quickly rejected the thought. I ought to explain to her, make her understand me, and above all make her recognize me. Because, for a long time now, when she spoke to him it was as if she were addressing a stranger, a hostile stranger whom Louis did not know any more than she did, and whom he could never have liked or put up with. She had substituted for the loving, trusting, cheery Louis he had known himself to be, a snobbish, remote clod. He at least had never forgotten the charming, happy girl, the sincere woman she had once been and with whom he had never stopped trying to communicate. And it was with an astonished and grief-stricken tenderness that he became aware of her refusal to listen to him. She, on the other hand, found a bitter, intellectual pleasure in stripping away the mask of what she took to be his real self. Perhaps neither of them any longer resembled the image each had created of the other and had loved. But he, at least, did not repudiate her; he at least regretted losing the person she had once been! At least his complaint was that he was no longer happy, whereas she complained of never having been so. Opening his eyes in the dark, he thought that it was probably because he really had loved that woman and that he truly missed her that he would be able to leave her. Something she would never be able to do. If he were to leave her, it would be in remembrance of her.

The voice up there above him, sounding far away, ranted on: "You know, Louis, words can do a lot of harm. We'll have to be careful. You must never again tell me anything you don't really believe," she added seriously, "even in anger, It leaves a scar, you know. . . . Are you listening?"

But he was no longer listening. He would never again listen to her. He had closed his eyes once more and what he listened to instead was the whistling of a bicyclist in the deserted street. Soon it would be his own tune, he thought to himself, that some free man—perhaps he himself—would whistle at dawn in a street like this one.

Third Person Singular

The day after his marriage, Lucas Ambrieu was worried about his future. His happiness may well have seemed assured to everyone else; but it did not seem so to his tormented spirit. He had vowed to make Laurence happy. He had vowed it to her parents, to her entire family, to her friends, even to her, not to mention her former suitors. But he had neither seen nor heard Laurence make the same commitment to his nearest and dearest. Actually, he no longer had any family, but he did have devoted men friends and doting women friends. Laurence, for her part, had promised them nothing. And yet, for example, what did she think Marie-Claire—dear old Marie-Claire, one of Lucas's marriage witnesses —had meant when she said: "You're going to civilize this good-for-nothing, aren't you, Laurence? You're going to knock some sense into him? But of course, you won't overdo it?" What did that mean to anyone with sense except: You must look after him. You must not force him into the mold of an upper-echelon executive, or allow him to take himself too seriously? Yet when Jerome, his childhood friend, had laughingly groaned, "What a relief to hand this old rake over to you, Laurence. . . . I've just about had it losing him in nightclubs for weeks on end," surely, decoded, that meant: Love him, cherish him; he's a big baby. But give him enough leeway to make him think he is free.

"Yes, yes, I'll take over. I don't know if I'll succeed, but I'll do what I can," Laurence had replied, also laughing.

Lucas had not liked that last statement, that "I'll do what I can"—as though there were a limit to Laurence's powers, a limit to the strength of a woman in love. And yet, she was in love. It was she who had wanted the marriage. It was she who had wept when he'd offered to give it up. It could not possibly have been ambition on her part: After all, Lucas was only a minor PR man whose business wasn't exactly puny, but nothing to compare with his in-laws, for instance. Laurence's father headed the four biggest flour mills in France.

Third Person Singular

Yes, she did love him. She was ready to devote the "best years of her life" to him; but would these also be the "best years" for Lucas? He was forty-five, and the best years of his life so far had been, at sixteen, his discovery of "woman," while celebrating his graduation; at thirty-two, his discovery of "a woman," when he met and married the love of his life; and finally, at forty, his discovery of "women," when he had divorced the love of his life.

Laurence was only twenty-five and he was her first man, if not her first lover.

Nonetheless, despite her love for him, it was clear that Lucas's happiness was not Laurence's sole concern (a man's happiness was not, as a rule, the sole concern of any twenty-five-year-old woman in love). But on the other hand, her chief concern was not her own happiness either, even if at her age, such a thing would have been quite understandable. But it was not so, not at all! Laurence plainly obeyed laws other than the laws of love; she sometimes wore a determined, calm little air as she went off to her dressmaker or to a fashionable dinner party—an air of stubborn tranquillity that seemed to spring from a sense of duty well done. (Or of despair? But this she was still unfamiliar with.) Marital duty, thank heavens, was not looked upon by her as a duty. Nor was running the house, since it was admirably run by Melinda, the trusty housekeeper who was guided by Lucas's mother-in-law from the confines of Avenue Foch. Nor was it the few hours she spent at l'Ecole du Louvre.

What was it then, this quality she possessed when she was in evening clothes at a fancy nightclub or in her cashmere coat at Longchamps (the Longchamps races were the only ones to which she went, to Lucas's sorrow), or even when she was lounging at home in her blue jeans, in the big house with the small garden she had found in l'Alma. . . . What was it that conferred upon her that look of triumphant virtue? It was a look that only Lucas could detect. No one else could see or define it (Marie-Claire could have, perhaps, but she was spending a year in Mexico). It was a look that could easily have been ascribed to self-assurance, happiness, gaiety, coquetry, character, even irony; but he knew that it came from something else, something very close to smugness—but not that, thank God (otherwise, he would certainly not have married her), for she was sometimes ashamed of herself, of the way she looked, of the sort of person she was.

It was with these gloomy questions floating through his weary mind that Lucas drove home. Once parked, he closed the garden gate behind his car and walked to the porch. The part-time gardener, hired of course through Avenue Foch, was cutting flowers that went by names unknown to Lucas. Since his acquaintance with botany was limited to poppies, roses, and tulips, Lucas had intended to pass him by with a simpleminded but admiring smile, but just then the man straightened up. He was short, old, and looked as if he belonged on the stage: Lucas's mother-in-law had always had servants who were like caricatures of themselves, bordering nearly on satire. It was not just her staff, thought Lucas: friends, associates, his entire family of in-laws (with the exception, of course, of Laurence) were a ferocious parody of the moneyed middle class.

"Good day," said the gardener, removing his cap.

He ought to have added "Master," thought Lucas. "Hello!" he replied pleasantly. "How goes it?"

"Oh, so-so," the man said with a worried air.

Lucas put his weight on his right foot and said in a conciliatory voice: "Can I help?"

"Yes, he can," Lucas thought he heard, and listened more closely.

"Does he think this is pretty?"

Lucas turned around; they were alone. "Who?" he asked.

"Gosh, him." The gardener was pointing his earth-stained finger at Lucas.

"Me?" asked Lucas, surprised. "Yes, I like it; it's very pretty." So, the worthy old gardener was not quite right in the head: stress was an occupational hazard even in such peaceable, age-old pursuits as the working of the soil.

"I was thinking," the man went on, "if he

wants to keep those bushes, I'll keep them for him, but if he'd prefer flower beds, I could easily manage that for him."

Lucas shifted his weight to the other foot and hesitated. "Listen," he said gently, "if you're talking about me, I like all flowers. I'm not crazy about bushes, but it's my wife who makes the decisions. Settle it with her." He turned on his heel as the gardener was putting his cap back on his head, muttering, "Good, tomorrow I'll ask his wife."

Lucas smiled. He would have reported this conversation to Laurence right away if she had not been in the bath when he arrived. She emerged from it ten minutes later and showered him with kisses. They dined at the house of some friends of hers, crashingly dull but fashionable Americans with whom, in any event, Lucas expected to make a fabulous deal. It was only later that night when she was lying naked beside him that he told her about the gardener.

"Oh," she said in a faint voice, "Philibert? Poor Philbert!"

"You mean to tell me his name is Philibert?!" exclaimed Lucas ecstatically.

"He comes from the country and I had his wife explain to him that he was to address us in the third person, but I didn't succeed. He does use the third person, but he says "he" and "she" instead of "Monsieur" and "Madame.""

"Oh, so that's it! And why are you so keen on having him address us in the third person?" He asked the question idly, just to say something, so as not to lose contact with that body with which he felt such an immense kinship after their recent passionate lovemaking.

"As my mother says," replied Laurence sleepily but not without a measure of filial pride, "if you want to do the dishes yourself, go ahead; but if you feed and pay people to do them for you, then they must keep their distance."

"If it's a toss-up between saying: 'Lucas, do you like tulips?' and 'Does Monsieur like tulips . . .' " he began, but Laurence was already asleep.

Lucas too fell asleep, but he was disquieted. He did not like the false aphorisms (even if they were her mother's) with which Laurence so readily clothed her outbursts of insincerity.

A few days later, having completely forgotten the gardener, Lucas was surprised to have him open the car door, head bowed, kneading his beret with hands that were undoubtedly calloused.

Lucas had spent a hard day with a manufacturer who had no taste, and he directed a hostile look at the poor man, who lowered his eyes and bent down. Lucas made an effort. "And so, my dear Philibert," (he miraculously remembered the man's name) "is everything all right? It's going to be beautiful."

"Didn't she tell him?"

The sibylline quality of the question was enhanced by his dramatic tone. It could easily have been: "Did Andromache not tell him that Hector is dead?"

"She didn't tell him . . . what didn't she tell me? Who? *Mad*—my wife?" Lucas blushed; he had almost said "Madame."

"His wife, yes," answered Philibert; he was having no trouble now keeping all these grammatical characters straight. "She said nothing to him?"

"No," Lucas said prudently. "No."

"Well, she ought to have," the gardener retorted in a voice of unaccustomed authority. "Because if the soil isn't turned under they won't have anything to look at this spring. About the only thing I can plant in this compost pile is ivy."

"Well then, turn it under for her," said Lucas, moving off, struggling wildly to smother the waves of laughter rising within him.

He went to Laurence's room, eyes streaming, and tried to explain why he was laughing but, when he succeeded, she did not laugh; in fact, she even appeared to be exasperated. Lucas calmed down quickly, but he was nonetheless able to discern his wife's pinched look, the thin line of her mouth, and the sudden frightening resemblance to her mother.

"It isn't funny, you know. Melinda and I are having a hard enough time teaching those people some manners. If his wife didn't cook so divinely, I'd already have fired the idiot."

"Well, go ahead," he said with a laugh, thinking she was joking. "Then on Sundays I can prune the roses."

"In your shirt sleeves, with a jug of red wine on the porch, is that it? So that our neighbors can behold *a man of the people?*"

"But . . ." said Lucas, stunned, "what on earth is the matter with you?"

A little later, she got all worked up, wept, claimed she was jumpy and depressed, and they made it up in bed. But the knell had tolled for Lucas. He understood now. He had the answer to his questions: Laurence was a snob.

A few months later, night had already fallen when Lucas went home, for it was now November. The house was dark except for the kitchen window, but Lucas whistled. He was about to sell the house: it was much too large for a single man. The word "single" had become synonymous with "delight" after months of mutual exasperation. Ah, his name must have been mud at Avenue Foch.

The rustic in charge of the garden was there, as he usually was on Tuesdays, Thursdays, and Saturdays. He had been digging effortlessly, as though he too had grown younger since the departure of Laurence.

"There he is," he said to Lucas. "Gosh, he's

FRANÇOISE SAGAN

not going to be pleased. I wanted to dig up her begonias, which he didn't like, but I pulled up the Japanese apple tree. We'll have to get two new apple trees, but it's not right for him to pay for them."

"Never mind," Lucas said, "he'll pay for them anyway."

"Well, I thought, he's going to be hopping mad. Japanese apple trees cost a lot. I've been saying to myself all afternoon, 'What's he going to say?'"

He followed Lucas to the porch and shouted warmly, "Martha! It's him!"

The house smelled of fried chicken and cigars. Lucas had had a wonderful poker game the night before with the boys.

"He's sure he's not mad at me?" Philibert persisted.

"That's easy," Lucas stated firmly. "If he says anything to you, you must tell me and I'll throw him out." And turning to the mystified man, he added: "Isn't that right? We can't let them bully us, her and him?" And he went into his large, silent, and exquisite house, laughing to himself.